I0678009

THE WIZARD OF BERNER'S ABBEY

And MONK'S TOWER

Mark Hansom

RAMBLE HOUSE

The Wizard of Berner's Abbey ©1935 by Mark Hansom
Introduction © 2009 by John Pelan
This edition © 2009 by Ramble House

ISBN 13: 978-1-60543-404-9

ISBN 10: 1-60543-404-3

Cover Art: Gavin L. O'Keefe
Preparation: Fender Tucker

DANCING TUATARA PRESS #5

THE WIZARD OF WRIGHT & BROWN

Welcome! Since you've tracked this book down, we have to assume that you are familiar with either (a) the work of Mark Hansom, (b) my work as an editor when it comes to bringing obscure works of mystery or the supernatural back into print, or (c) you were browsing the Ramble House site and saw Gavin O'Keefe's remarkably cool cover for this book and decided to take a chance on it.

This volume is the third Mark Hansom title to be released by Dancing Tuatara Press and the fourth of his seven novels to be resurrected under my editorship (the fourth, *The Beasts of Brahm* was published by Midnight House and is still available, e-mail jpelan6@msn.com for ordering information.) If this is your first Mark Hansom book, you're starting with the book I consider the most typical of his novels and in many respects, one of his best. There's some difference of opinion on this, of course. The late Karl Edward Wagner cited Hansom's first book, *The Shadow on the House* (also available from Ramble House) as his best book, naming it one of the thirteen best non-supernatural horror novels. However, even this is open to debate as Karl admitted to me that at the time he composed his list, *The Shadow on the House* was the only Hansom book he had encountered at the time. Karl later went on to acquire all of Hansom's novels, but I never did get a chance to find out whether or not he had revised his opinion.

While Hansom's first novel was a masterpiece of psychological horror, with his two 1935 novels, (*The Ghost of Gaston Revere* and *The Wizard of Berner's Abbey*) Hansom leaped into the supernatural genre with both feet. In both books Hansom uses a motif that became his hallmark: the antagonist perishes early on in the story only to prove far more baleful an influence from beyond the grave. In *The*

Wizard of Berner's Abbey, we learn enough of Paul St. Arnaud and his experiments using the power of the human will to know that he's a formidable individual and the hero of the piece, a young medical student would seem to be horribly overmatched. Then to our surprise, St. Arnaud collapses from pneumonia and dies and would thus seem to be incapable of inflicting harm or even annoying anyone . . . But then we wouldn't have much of a story, would we?

I can't reveal much more without spoiling things, so I'll leave it to you to find out whether or not Paul St. Arnaud is a wizard capable of enforcing his will on the living from beyond the grave, or a run-of-the-mill mad scientist. Suffice it to say, there are a number of surprises and Hansom's pacing makes the book a real page-turner.

Added to this volume is a bonus, the first publication since 1939 of Hansom's only known short story, "Monk's Tower". Once again, Hansom defies convention; whereas most authors begin their career's writing short fiction before tackling a novel, Hansom ends his career with a short story. Whether this was intentional or not is unknown as we shall see . . .

So who was this inventive and vastly entertaining author, and why did he stop writing in 1939? The fact of the matter is that no one really knows for certain . . . Even though I was responsible for his entry in the encyclopaedia *Supernatural Literature of the World,* I was unable to include more than a brief bibliography and some conjectures as to what may have become of him . . .

We do know that "Mark Hansom" was a pseudonym; there are no records of a person with that name being born (or dying) in the United Kingdom that could possibly have been the author. The man writing as Mark Hansom began his career in 1934 and his career ended almost to the day that Great Britain entered the Second World War. Assuming that he was a young man in mid-to-late twenties at the time it's not at all unreasonable to think that he may have died in the service of his country.

Another possibility is that "Hansom" was the pseudonym for another author working the field, or possibly someone employed in some capacity at Wright & Brown. What suggests this possibility is the program of reprinting abridged versions of his novels undertaken by Mellifont in the 1950s. Certainly it's possible that a contract was entered into by his heirs, but considering the extensive revisions done it would seem more likely that Mellifont had a living author to work with.

There have been a few theories as to the identity behind the pseudonym, and please keep in mind that it's much easier to poke holes in other scholars work than it is to come up with one's own hypothesis. Richard Dalby proposed that "Mark Hansom" was yet another pseudonym for Charles Cannell, better known to most of us as "E. Charles Vivian" or "Jack Mann". There are some fairly obvious flaws in this line of thought, not the least of which is an extreme stylistic difference. Now Cannell was able to vary his style, the "Gees" novels are quite unlike his work as "Vivian". However, one central motif that runs through all of his and that is a fascination with aviation. If Cannell's characters need to get from point A to point B by air, Cannell gave you a through description of the type of airplane involved, details of its capacity, mechanics, etc. If Hansom needed to move people about, a cursory line or two would be the extent of his description. Another point of difference is that Hansom seemed very well acquainted with the lifestyle of the upper class, so much so in fact that I strongly suspect that he was a member of it. There doesn't seem to be much of this class-consciousness in any of Cannell's work. There are other differences, but just on the strength of these two points I would be inclined to reject Dalby's theory.

A number of people have put forth the idea that "Mark Hansom" was the same person masquerading behind the rather obvious pseudonym of "Rex Dark". On the surface, this seems quite a bit more plausible as both authors were active at almost exactly the same time and both stopped writing (at least under these names) at almost exactly the same time. However, while the similarity in careers (Hansom: 1934-1939) and (Dark: 1936-1940) on which this theory is based seems to me to be the strongest argument *against* its viability. The idea that an author energetic enough to churn out seventeen novels in seven years would just seemingly vanish is enough to raise eyebrows. This line of reason would certainly be in keeping with the theory that the author perished in the early days of WWII.

On the surface this looks pretty plausible; the only rebuttal that I can offer is based on numerous readings of the Hansom novels and reading two of the Rex Dark books. (Whoever he was, "Rex Dark's" novels seem to be almost as elusive as "Mark Hansom's). All I can say is that the stylistic differences seem very pronounced. Unlike the case with Cannell I can't easily point to one or two items, it's more of a case of a pronounced difference in sentence structure, dialogue, pacing, plotting. To me, it's much like placing a story by M.R. James next to a tale by Lovecraft; one needn't be a literary detective to readily ascertain that two different people wrote the stories. The comparison of "Mark Hansom" and "Rex Dark" seems to be equally obvious.

So there we are, we can say pretty definitely that we know who "Mark Hansom" wasn't, but we aren't left with any but a few tantalizing clues as to who he may have been. I'm pretty solidly convinced that he was likely a young man of the upper class, (his references to the first World War are those of a man too young to have been directly involved). Very likely Wright & Brown employed him in some capacity; (the publishing business was deemed suitable for young men of the upper class to get a taste of the business world before returning to manage the family's affairs. An example would be Sir Charles Birkin putting in a stint at Philip Allan as an editor.) Equally likely is that he was killed in the war. I've previously considered the idea that he survived the war and wound up working with Mellifont based on their reprinting of his work, but the abridged editions are so ham-fistedly done that I can't imagine a living author condoning the messes that were made of the two novels that they butchered

(The Shadow on the House and *The Ghost of Gaston Revere)*. Also, the more I investigated, the more books from Wright & Brown I discovered having been picked up for reprint by Mellifont, so the case of Mellifont reprinting Hansom and Dark was far from unique.

Perhaps at some point we'll discover the identity of the man (or woman) behind the Mark Hansom name; in the meantime we have seven exciting novels to enjoy!

John Pelan
Midnight House

THE WIZARD OF
BERNER'S ABBEY

CHAPTER I

IN THE WOOD

IT WAS A WARM EVENING IN LATE AUGUST. I was making my way across country to that queerly named and queerly fashioned mansion, Berner's Abbey; and though I could never think of Berner's Abbey without a certain feeling of uneasiness, I was, on this particular evening, in normally pleasant spirits and had no forebodings of calamity. Least of all did I expect to meet with experiences of such profound horror as would affect my thoughts for months afterwards, causing me to be acutely aware of the vast and sinister world that lies just beyond everyday human consciousness.

I had not been invited to Berner's Abbey and my visit was unheralded. To wait for an invitation would be to spend years in vain waiting, and to announce my intention of calling would be to receive a note or a telegram saying that the inhabitants of the place were just on the point of going off on holiday. I had formerly taken the trouble to ask on several occasions whether I might pay them a flying visit and had been put off with one excuse or another and in consequence I was now wiser and had adopted the surer plan of simply ringing the bell at the front door and stepping inside.

The great fact behind this piece of minor intrigue was the fact that I was in love with Leonora St. Arnaud. Leonora was twenty-three, and two years earlier she had married the middle-aged Paul St. Arnaud. It had been all but settled that she should marry me, and it took me a good few months to recover even partially from the shock of learning that she intended to marry St. Arnaud—that she had indeed married St. Arnaud.

I was only a year her senior—young enough, some might say, to get over a disappointment of that sort. But I had not got over it. The intense love that I felt for Leonora would have survived a dozen marriages to a dozen St. Arnauds, and it was thus that I still hankered after her company and descended to minor intrigue in order to see her occasionally.

I pressed the point that she was my cousin, though the relationship was purely a bit of conceit which depended on nothing stronger than the marriage of two distant relatives of ours. It was in order to justify myself in the eyes of her husband that I maintained this fiction, for otherwise it would be impossible for even a strong-headed young fellow of twenty-four, who was a rejected suitor, to continue paying attentions to a married woman.

But I could not imagine Leonora as a married woman. Nor could I imagine myself as a rejected suitor. She did not love Paul St. Arnaud; I was sure of that. I was equally sure that she still loved me. And though these convictions were apparently rendered foolish by the actual facts of the case, I still clung to them, believing that some undue influence must have been exercised in bringing about the marriage, and hoping that the time might come when events would allow my constancy to be rewarded.

Of the undue influences that might have forced the marriage I knew nothing definitely; I reasoned merely from my knowledge of Leonora and from my knowledge of her husband. But that there had been coercion of some sort I was positive, for Leonora would never have allied herself of her own free will with a man like Paul St. Arnaud—a man thirty years her senior and one who was completely absorbed to scientific inquiry and who was no companion for a naturally healthy and vivacious girl.

Of the nature of the influence that had caused her to reject me and accept him I was soon to learn; and, learning that, I was to be faced with a state of affairs of such horrible significance that even I, a student of medicine could not but stand aghast.

At the moment, however, these thoughts did not worry me. I was concerned only with reaching Berner's Abbey before I should be overtaken by the storm clouds that were gathering swiftly from the horizon.

I was not weather-wise. When I stepped out from the little station of Bernersleigh it never occurred to me to look for a conveyance of any sort in the village. The journey down from London had been slow and tedious—for no fast trains stop at Bernersleigh—and by the time I found myself standing in the almost deserted street of the little Surrey village I was ready for a walk and a breath of Surrey air.

Therefore it was that I chose to walk two miles through woods and by field-paths in preference to hunting up a car of some sort that would take me rattling and bumping round the three or four miles of road that lay between me and Berner's Abbey.

I had left my suitcase at the station, after being assured that it would not be delivered at Berner's Abbey until at least an hour later. I did not want my case to arrive before I did, for that would give them warning of my approach and would give them time to invent a story that would send me away again the next morning. I wanted to take them by surprise and, insisting on the cousinly relationship between Leonora and myself, I wanted to tell them that I intended to inflict my company upon them for a whole week. Cousins, 1 reflected, could take such liberties with each other.

It was when I had left the main road by the first stile and was half-way across the first field that I became aware of a change to the atmosphere. The air, all along, had been heavy, and had I thought to study the weather I should have known that we were in for a thunderstorm; but by now I was going at a good round pace and reckoned upon reaching Berner's Abbey before the storm broke.

Although it was not much after six o'clock, a decided darkness had begun to fall. In truth, it was not so much a darkness as a kind of grey light—an eerie, unreal twilight that gave a sinister appearance to everything it touched. And this sense of the unreal and the sinister was further impressed upon me by the utter stillness of the air and by the heaviness that lay on me like a pall.

These were the normal conditions preceding a thunderstorm, but to me then—probably because of the loneliness of the countryside through which I was passing—they took on a supernatural quality, and I found myself speculating upon the power of matter over mind and delving into questions of psychology—a subject of which I was a student though, I fear, a backward one.

The path now led me into a thick wood. This wood was the haunt of gloom even at midday in summer. Now it was dark and hot and still. It was such a wood as might figure in a superstitious people's folklore; and as I entered it I impulsively checked my haste and walked cautiously, having the feeling that its deepest shadows held things sinister and stealthy.

This wood is the best part of half a mile across and it was while I was in the midst of this plague-spot of fear that the storm actually broke. It broke with one big flash of lightning, followed, at barely a second's interval, by a crash of thunder. And the crash of thunder was accompanied by a scream that made me stop abruptly, and, in fact, that made me take a step backwards on the path.

For a moment I was dazed by the sudden burst of light and by the sudden blood-curdling sounds—dazed or startled into inactivity, I know not which. And in the utter silence which followed I recovered some of my composure and stood listening for some further human sound that would help me to fix the direction from which the scream had come, but all around me was only the brooding silence of the trees.

Then I shrugged my shoulders—just as though there had been someone with me. I might have laughed; I can't remember whether I did or not. But I know that there occurred to me the thought that my imagination had been playing me false and that the thunder and the flash of the lightning had, between them, startled me into hearing a shriek that had not actually occurred. I was somewhat ashamed of having shown fear, and I remember with what deliberation I stayed to put on my raincoat and to put the collar up about my neck.

And yet, I thought, I could not have imagined that shriek. Why should I imagine a shriek? Why should it not be an actual shriek? I asked myself these questions as I put the final touches to my raincoat and hurried forward.

There had been nothing to indicate the direction from which the shriek—assuming it to be real—had come. It had been so confused with the double crack of the thunder that it had been impossible to place its direction. I started to run, wondering whether I should alight on any explanation of the unholy sound. For perhaps fifty yards I ran forward, then I stopped to listen. But there was nothing to be heard except the pitter-patter of the first raindrops and nothing to be seen except the eerie light that cast its spell over the countryside and which even penetrated to the clearings of this gloomy wood.

That shriek was still echoing through my brain, and every ten yards or so I stopped to listen. I wondered whether I ought not to make some sort of a search, and I was debating this point when it occurred to me that perhaps a pair of lovers were in the wood and that the first flash of lightning had made the girl shriek with fright.

In any case, I did not make any attempt at a search. Perhaps it was as well that I did not for I might have been led far away from the path and might not have learnt what I did learn.

I was only a few yards from the edge of the wood and was right glad to see the open country and the twin towers of Berner's Abbey nestling darkly in the woods on the other side of the valley, when I heard a crackling of undergrowth near at hand. I stopped dead in my tracks, and almost immediately a man in headlong flight broke through a thicket some yards in front of me and set off down the path towards the open fields.

Instinctively I gave chase. Really, I could not make his flight any business of mine, but I gave chase. I even called to

him. He either did not hear my calls or else he purposely ignored them.

There were one or two features about this man that struck
me immediately. One was the recklessness of his speed along
a path made dangerous by the outgrowing roots of trees and
now made slippery by the rain that was pouring off the overhanging branches. A second feature, more surprising than the
first, was the fact that he was in evening dress—that is to say
he wore a dinner-jacket and I had caught the flash of white at
his chest when he struggled through the thicket. And still another noticeable feature was that he carried what appeared to
be a small package in one hand.

There is nothing unusual in anybody carrying a small
package, but this man carried the package with such care—
holding it away from his body as one might carry a glass of
water—that he actually hampered his own progress.

All the circumstances of his appearance—especially his
being in a wood as lonely as this wood, and in the midst of a
thunderstorm, and being dressed in a dinner-jacket—were
very odd and made me wish to see more of him.

I was gaining rapidly and knew that I should easily catch
up with him when he reached the open. In the meantime I
had to run with care because of the treacherous path.

We reached the open and I put on a big spurt, shouting,
meanwhile, to attract his attention.

He apparently did not hear me, for he neither slackened
his speed nor increased it; and it was not until I was abreast
of him that he seemed to be aware of my presence.

Then he checked himself abruptly and, at the risk of going slithering head over heels turned and faced me, at the
same time emitting an exclamation of impatience that had
about it the quality of a snarl.

I stepped back instinctively—not in preparation to defend
myself, though that motive might have been justified by the
wildly aggressive look on his face—but in complete surprise;
for the man who stood literally trembling before me was
Leonora's husband, Paul St. Arnaud.

CHAPTER II

THE MYSTERIOUS RESPONSE

FOR A FULL TEN SECONDS we stood looking at each other, St. Arnaud and I. There had never been much sympathy between us; for how could I even with the best intentions in the world, be other than inimical towards one who had stepped between me and supreme happiness? And for his part, though he was to the best of my knowledge unaware of the tender relations that had existed between Leonora and me, he seemed to regard me as a disturbing element in his life. I doubt not but that he would long ago have forbidden me the premises had I not claimed Leonora as my cousin. He bore with me, but that was all.

Thus, for a full ten seconds, we stood looking at each other.

I had long known, of course, that St. Arnaud was queer in his habits. That is to say, I had known that for days at a stretch he would shut himself up in his laboratory in the western wing of the house and have his food sent to him. But of many scientists similar peculiarities may be related for it seems that scientific research is an all absorbing matter, and when the solution of some problem is in sight the scientist has no patience to attend to the ordinary affairs of life.

But I had never suspected St. Arnaud of more than the normal scientist's enthusiasm. And here was more than the normal scientist's enthusiasm, if I could read a man's eyes with any accuracy.

In my medical work—though I was still the merest tyro of a student—I had become acquainted with madness in more than one form and as I looked into St. Arnaud's eyes, I feared, if I could not actually predicate, that his enthusiasm had gone beyond the ordinary bounds and had become that dangerous quality that is just a step farther than genius—that quality that sets at naught everything but the subject's own aims. In this state the subject seems to lose all moral sense. Nothing matters but the work on which he is engaged. Life itself is not held sacred; nor, of course, is human or brute suffering; and he will inflict the most indescribable pain or will send a soul to its last home as calmly as he will put fluid into a test-tube.

And that, I suspected, was the condition of the man who stood before me in the darkening countryside.

"I'm afraid I startled you," I said, by way of suggesting that though I had noticed his agitation I had put it down to an ordinary cause.

"Startled me!" he exclaimed, turning and continuing on his way. "Yes. You startled me. That was it. You startled me."

I fell in beside him.

He, however, seemed to ignore my presence, and after a few yards was again breaking into a run. His eyes had a frightful unseeing expression about them and remained fixed on a point far ahead. The hand that held the package—which 1 now made out to be something wrapped hurriedly in brown paper—was stretched out as before.

"You got caught in the rain?" I remarked.

The remark was somewhat lacking in originality, for by this time we were both soaked to the skin. I know that I was soaked to the skin and I had a so-called raincoat for protection, but his plight looked even worse than mine, for besides having no raincoat he had no hat, and his fine clothes were simply a wet mass.

"Yes," he said, speaking absently, it seemed, "I was caught in the rain."

"Is Leonora well?" I next hazarded.

At that he stopped again and looked at me, and I could see that until now he had not been aware of my identity.

"Richmond!" he exclaimed. "What the devil are you doing here, Richmond?"

"I've just run down to see my cousin," I answered. "She's quite well, is she?"

"Of course she's quite well," he replied. "Why shouldn't she be quite well? What were you doing in that wood?"

He was still staring into my face. It was obvious that my presence was not welcome to him. It never had been very welcome to him but now I had the impression that he regarded me as a dangerous intruder. His gaze suggested that impression. He seemed to be trying to read my thoughts and to be speculating upon the accident of my finding him in headlong flight from the wood.

And, in truth, that is just what I was speculating upon. The shriek of terror and his sudden appearance were enough to set up the wildest speculations.

"It's the nearest way to Berner's Abbey," I said in reply to his last question. Then as we started forward again—at a walk now, for we had reached the bottom of the valley and were faced with a climb up towards the house—I shot my bolt.

"Did you hear a scream?" I asked.

"No," he said promptly.

"When the first crash of thunder came," I proceeded "I thought I heard a scream. You must have heard it too, surely," I added, daring much in making such a suggestion.

"I tell you I did not," he asserted fiercely. "But if I did, what of it? Somebody afraid of the lightning, no doubt."

Although this explanation seemed feasible enough and had, indeed, occurred to me earlier, I could not help thinking that St. Arnaud did know something about the shriek.

"I have a good mind," I said, "to go back and see whether there is anything wrong. Somebody might have been struck by the lightning."

"We should have heard before now if there were anything wrong," he replied. "If somebody were struck, that somebody could not have shrieked. It must have been the survivor who shrieked, and he or she would certainly have continued to shout in order to attract the attention of anybody who might be passing. No doubt you imagined it," he concluded.

I was only too ready to fall in with this explanation, for there are few discomforts so unpleasant as that of being thoroughly wet through, and I was eager above all things to reach Berner's Abbey and change into some dry clothes.

And St. Arnaud, now that I had drawn his mind away from whatever problem had been claiming its whole attention, had lost his wild agitation and was talking like any normal being.

"I had an hour to spare before dinner," he told me "so I went hunting for specimens. I changed first so that I would know how much actual time I had to spare. That is why you find me in this dress."

"Specimens?" I echoed. "What sort of specimens, may I ask?"

"Well—" he said, and paused.

"Animal, vegetable, or mineral?" I pursued.

I saw him turn his head and glance at me.

"Oh, vegetable, of course!" he said, and he added quickly: "Leonora will be pleased to see you."

I understood that he did not wish me to question him on the specimens he had been procuring and which he held so carefully in that little brown-paper parcel.

"She won't be very pleased to see me in this condition," I replied, "She will have to wait until I've changed. And a hot bath won't do either of us any harm. We don't want to go and catch pneumonia. You have two bathrooms in going order, I suppose?"

I asked the question incidentally, but I remembered that when I was last at Berner's Abbey the greater part of the huge mansion had been shut up and only a few rooms in the main part of the building left in use. Leonora had complained to me at the time that her husband was gradually closing the place and that he had cut down the domestic staff to only two or three. And I remember thinking at the time that if she allowed him to give way to his desire for seclusion she might end up by finding herself entirely alone with him in the house. And that would be an unspeakably dull life for a girl like Leonora. I did not think of it as being anything worse than dull. I never imagined that Leonora would be forced to go through such an existence of horror as I was soon to hear about.

"No," he said; "there's only one bathroom in use, I think. I don't know. But it doesn't matter. You have a bath. I shan't have time to change immediately."

"But you must change," I told him. "You mustn't risk wearing those wet clothes a minute longer than is necessary."

"Ah!" he exclaimed, and the exclamation was something of a sneer. "I shan't come to any harm. You, as a medical student, should know that the will can keep one immune from physical disorders."

I, as a medical student, did not know that the will could keep one immune from physical disorders; but I did not say so.

"The will" he went on "can control everything. There is nothing greater than will. Life—death itself—can be made subject to one's will."

I thought he was rambling, therefore I made no comment. I had previously met people who had speculated at length on just what the will might actually be capable of, and had listened to some of the wildest discourses on the possibility of an after life in which the will figured as the central source of existence. Among the more original of my medical student friends I had heard it stated seriously that by a very intensive training of the will one could keep in touch with this world after death. But among the more original of my medical student friends I had heard a great deal of nonsense spoken at one time or another. I had paid no attention to it. And I was not going to pay attention to the present ramblings of Paul St. Arnaud.

"Well," I said lightly, "whatever you might think about it, I'm going to have a hot bath whenever I get indoors, and by that time my case will probably have arrived from the station, so that I'll be able to get into some dry things."

"Your case?" said St. Arnaud. "Are you staying, then?"

I told him I was. I said I had not seen my dear cousin for months, which was quite true, and that I intended to plant myself upon them for a whole week.

"But you can't stay," he exclaimed. "It will be most inconvenient. I mean there will be nothing for you to do. I mean, Leonora and I are very deeply engaged in my work just now. I take up her whole time. She will have none to spare for entertaining. No, no! You mustn't think of staying."

I could trace in his voice a return of his former agitation. It was obvious that he was concerned about something deeper than the question of a guest's comfort. It would not have mattered to him whether I should find entertainment or not. There was another reason for his wishing me not to stay, and that reason, I guessed, had to do with something that was not quite open and above board in his life—had to do with that queerness of which I had always been aware. I knew that there was some sort of a mystery about Berner's Abbey, and the present strange attitude of Paul St. Arnaud hinted to me that the mystery might possibly be brought to light and confirmed me in my intention to stay for as long as I possibly could.

If his experiments were innocent experiments, I reasoned, he could have no objection to my being about the place. I guessed that they were not innocent, and as we took the last slope towards the house, which now stood out black against the sky, I was searching my mind for an incontestable argument for my staying, and had come to the conclusion that I should just stay and should adopt an attitude of blindness to any hints I might receive saying that my presence was not wanted.

But I need not have troubled myself with this point. Events transpired which made my presence in the house welcomed by those concerned.

The last few yards upwards lay through a little copse. The path was very steep and was so narrow that we had to walk singly. St. Arnaud preceded me. He was hurrying again as quickly as he could and I was labouring up behind him, having the utmost difficulty in following his strenuous pace.

I feared I was out of condition, but I was, nevertheless, amazed at the energy that he, a man of over fifty, could put forth, and I had to confess that, in spite of his age, he was physically superior to me.

Then he stumbled. We were nearing the top of the narrow path and, like one moved by an access of impatience, he started to run. One foot slipped and he was thrown with a thud to the ground. But instantly he was up again.

"Stop!" he shouted. "Don't move or—"

I stopped. He was mumbling to himself and had now got down on his knees and was groping about on the ground; and as he groped to this side and to that his mumbling became a whine, as though he were about to cry.

I perceived at once that he had dropped his brown-paper package in his fall; and I was surprised to hear his crying whine, thinking that a few botanical specimens that could be gathered less than a mile off in a matter of half an hour were not so important as to cause one to give way to tears of vexation.

Then something came tinkling down over the shingle towards me. I could not see what it was, but I put out my hand towards the sound and, after a moment's groping, picked up a glass container—perhaps about the size of a small tumbler—whose mouth was stopped by a large cork.

"Is this it?" I said; and as I held the container up, a flash of lightning illuminated the whole place for just about a second.

In that second I saw two things. The first was that the glass container held something reddish—or, at least, something lying in a reddish fluid. The second was the face of a madman being launched at me—a face of unspeakable fury.

Fortunately, I had my foot against a tree, and this gave me sufficient purchase to drive my free fist home to his jaw. It did not occur to me to drop the glass container that I held, but I should certainly have dropped it had a further onslaught been threatened. My blow however served to daze him and allay the extraordinary violence of his anger; and though he quickly recovered himself, he merely stepped forward, snatched the glass from my hand, and made off, whining or crying as before.

Then it was that perhaps the strangest thing of all happened.

I was almost by his side when he reached the top of the incline and emerged from the copse. Between the edge of the copse and the house there was a wide expanse of uncared-for lawns and overgrown gravel, so far as I could make out. And coming across this expanse, in a light dress and without any covering on her head, was Leonora.

It was her manner of walking that first struck me. She seemed to be unaware of the fact that the rain was simply lashing down and that her clothes must inevitably be soaked through in a matter of minutes; and she walked at a normal, unhurried pace, swinging her arms by her sides and looking this way and that—for all the world as though she were enjoying a stroll on a cool, fine evening.

She did not see us immediately, but continued to look this way and that. Then she stopped and called out.

"Paul!" she called. "Paul! I'm here. You called me. What do you want?"

St. Arnaud took not the slightest notice of her but, being now on level ground, set off at a brisk run towards the house, whose front was all in darkness, and disappeared within the main doorway.

As for me, I stood for a moment speechless, staring at the solitary figure standing in the middle of the dark lawns.

That it was Leonora I had not the least doubt. I knew her voice better than I knew any other voice in the world, and even in the half-light I could recognize her tall, slim figure and could even catch the suggestion of the wave in her fair hair.

It was her manner that rendered me speechless. Surely, I thought, no sane person could ignore rain such as this! But Leonora was apparently unaware of its existence. And she still continued to look for Paul, though in his race towards the house he had passed within a few feet of her so that she could not have failed to see him had she been in possession of her senses. And the most puzzling thing of all as her statement: "You called me." I had been with St. Arnaud all the way up from the valley and I was sure that he had never called her name. I was sure, also, that not one of our utterances could possibly have reached the house.

I ran towards her, startled, vaguely horrified.

"Leonora!" I exclaimed.

She took a step backwards, and gave a little scream. Then she seemed to recollect herself.

"John!" she said, holding out both her hands to me.

I was about to take them when she drew them back again.

"Why," she said, "you're all wet. You're wringing wet . . . Goodness, it's raining!"

And with that she turned quickly and ran towards the house, holding her hands over her hair.

I followed. I cannot describe my feelings, nor can I recall my exact thoughts. I was only aware of dark, unholy mystery.

CHAPTER III

A TELL-TALE HAND

L EONORA! When I first saw her clearly the light of the small drawing room at the back of the house to which she conducted me, I am afraid that I allowed my amazement to show in my face. I had not seen her for over two months, and my recollection of her was of a girl with the fine innocent bloom of youth upon her cheeks and the light of sparkling vitality in her eyes. And now I was shocked (I use the expression deliberately), I was shocked by the terrible change that had come over her.

Her face was a dead white, and the eyes that had once been so expressive and whose natural play had been not the least of her attractions were now dull and lifeless. The absence of that vivacity in her glance changed her whole expression, and as I stood before her trying to think of something commonplace to say, I had the feeling that I was looking upon a stranger. And most certainly I was not looking upon the Leonora with whom I had shared the first raptures of awakened love.

"I'm afraid I am spoiling your carpet," I said.

That was a sufficiently commonplace remark in all conscience and was prompted by my noticing that a wet stain was spreading outwards from where I stood.

I wanted to say ever so much more than that, but I did not dare to voice my thoughts in this the first moment of our reunion; for my thoughts—influenced by all that I had seen of St. Arnaud and by the strange behaviour and the emaciated appearance of Leonora—were delving amongst dark by-ways of conjecture—by-ways that seemed to lead to the very mysteries of the Pit.

She glanced carelessly at the water that was running off my clothes, and "It doesn't matter," she said in an unemotional voice.

Then suddenly she became more animated.

"Why did you come here?" she demanded, and for an instant her eyes flashed.

"To see my cousin," I replied as lightly as I could.

"You know I told you that you mustn't come here," she went on. "When you wrote from Paris last month I told you that you mustn't think of visiting me. I begged you to keep away."

"And why did you?" I asked her. "If you thought to damp my affection by forbidding me to see you, then you adopted a wrong course. But that probably wasn't your motive. I thought then that it was. But now I can't help thinking that it was something deeper than that."

"What do you mean?" she demanded sharply.

I had formerly been perfectly free from restraint in the presence of Leonora. She and I could discuss personal affairs with the ease inspired by deep mutual understanding, and even after her marriage with St. Arnaud I had maintained my old freedom. But now I felt a kind of diffidence and hesitated to touch upon the matters that were exercising my thoughts.

"You must know what I mean," I replied. "Your appearance, for one thing!" I ventured to say. "You aren't well."

"I am perfectly well," she asserted.

"No," I maintained, "you are not well. Your nerves are gone to the dickens."

She sat down on a settee and looked straight in front of her. I remained standing, forgetting for the moment that my first duty should be to change my wringing clothes.

"But that would be no reason for my forbidding you to come here," she said. "I tell you that you mustn't come here, and my reason for saying that is that it isn't right that you and I should continue to meet. I am married now, and I mustn't encourage you to think of me."

"Pardon me," I said, "but I think there's more in it than that. I'm sure there's more in it than that. If you will forgive me for saying so, I think there's something very queer about your husband. No, don't, say there isn't," I hurried to advise her, for she had turned towards me with a look of anger in her face. "I have seen enough to-night to convince me that things here are not normal—that there's some mystery about the place. That, I think, is the reason for your not wishing me to come here—some mystery."

"Mystery?" she echoed, with every appearance of innocent incomprehension. "What mystery should there be?"

I did not enlighten her. I did not speak of the curious circumstance in which I had found her husband in the wood, and I did not, of course, speak of the inexplicable manner in which she had come forth into the rain in answer to the call of a madman who, to my knowledge, had not summoned her—or who had not summoned her by any normal means, at least.

"Very well," I said, seeing that she did not intend to confide in me, "if you say that everything is all right, then I shan't worry. I'll run off and change. My suitcase will be arriving at any minute now, unless the carrier fellow has thought better about coming out here on a night like this."

She rose, looking at me queerly in the meantime.

"Your suitcase!" she said. "But you mustn't stay. I think Paul suspects that you and I have been more than cousins in the past. I'm sure he does. Please, John, don't make things more difficult for me! I hate to turn you away, but—"

"Oh, nonsense!" I replied, taking a cousinly liberty. "I know that Paul suspects nothing. And, anyway, there's nothing to suspect. No, Leonora, you must put up with me for a day or two."

I spoke lightly, purposely ignoring the expression of something very like fear that had come to her eyes. I thought it would be better for me not to insist too strongly on the presence of a mystery about Berner's Abbey. Leonora had refused to help me with any information. Not only that, but she had definitely tried to discourage my interest in the mystery and had finally attempted to send me away from the place altogether. That, of course, only made me the more anxious to stay and see what I could find out, and it made me careful not to exhibit my fears unnecessarily although I was afraid that I had already said too much.

She seemed to be about to utter a further protest against my staying, but I stopped her by drawing her attention to my dripping clothes.

"Shall I ring for somebody," I said, "who can find me a set of dry things? It looks as though the carrier has decided to take the evening off, though he promised me that he wouldn't fail to run my case round here."

"No," she said, "don't ring. I'll look something out for you."

And, picking up one of the brass lamps from the table, she preceded me into the hall and started to mount the huge staircase that is one of the dominating features of Berner's Abbey.

Until that moment I had not noticed that our conversation had been carried on by lamplight. The room in which we had been was a vast apartment—although I have referred to it as the small drawing-room—and though I had probably noticed it I had not been struck by the fact that most of the room had been in the shadow and that the sole light came from two oil-lamps on a table by one of the large windows.

But, seeing Leonora preceding me up the immense staircase, I now became aware of the absence of electricity.

"What's happened to the electric light plant?" I asked casually.

"Oh, it's—it's out of order, I think," she said.

The only thing that was clear in the gloom was the face of Leonora as she turned at the second gallery to wait for me to join her. She held the lamp breast-high; and its light was thrown upwards, giving to her features a ghastly glow, bringing her cheekbones into prominence and casting grisly shadows under her eyes.

It wanted but this to give the final expression to the uncanny atmosphere of the place. And though I knew it to be

Leonora who stood a foot or two above me on the gallery, I was assailed by a strange wave of fear. The shadows, thrown upwards. altered the whole cast of her features, making her face momentarily hideous. An instant later she was holding the lamp above her head and the death-like illusion had vanished. But it had affected me strangely, for I had been wondering whether Leonora's queerness of manner were due to some normal physical cause or whether it were a result of the dark mystery that I was sure was hanging over the house. I hardly dared to make my thoughts clearer at that moment, but I knew that I was ready to believe that she was on the verge of madness.

I had seen nothing of St. Arnaud since he raced across the lawns and disappeared within the dark hall. I assumed that he had gone immediately to his laboratory. But what struck me as most significant was that I had seen or heard nothing of anybody else in the huge mansion, with the exception, of course, of Leonora. And that fact, added to the strange circumstance of Leonora herself showing me upstairs and looking after my wants and the equally strange circumstance of there being only flickering oil-lamps to provide light, brought me to the conclusion that there was no one else on the premises.

I did not remark upon this. It would be as well, I thought, not to remark on anything unusual that I happened to notice; but I was very gravely concerned to think that the whole of the domestic staff—even the man who attended to the electric light plant—should have been dismissed. Whether it was that servants would not stay with St. Arnaud or whether it was that he had purposely dismissed them in order that he might conduct his experiments in complete privacy, I could not guess. At that moment I could only be fearfully aware of the terrible position of Leonora, who was shut away here in the uncanny deadness of this huge mansion with no one for company but a mad genius. For, by now, I had no doubt about his madness, and I never had had any doubt about his genius. And these two qualities made him more to be feared than the most violent homicidal maniac.

She led me into a bedroom, halfway along a corridor.

"You'll find everything you want here," she said. "There's a bathroom next door but one. Come down when you're ready. I'll leave you the lamp."

And before I could say a word she had gone. It had just occurred to me that I ought to have carried the lamp upstairs, and I was going to say as much; but she was gone, running along the corridor towards the main stairway. And as she ran I could hear her saying: "Yes, Paul, I'm coming!" And that struck me as inexplicable, for she had jumped suddenly into hasty activity at the moment of putting the lamp on the table, yet I had not heard a sound.

As I stood for a moment listening to the retreating footsteps of Leonora, I pictured the endless rooms stretching this way and that—rooms that were vaults of brooding silence, their furniture swathed in white dust-sheets, their dark recesses suggestive of unholy mysteries. And somewhere among these dead chambers was Paul St. Arnaud, engaged in his secret and, I guessed, iniquitous studies. And somewhere was Leonora.

No wonder that Leonora acted strangely! To me it seemed impossible that one could live long in this atmosphere of shadows and silent vaults without being affected by it. And when one realized that she was living in this atmosphere with a man who was capable of committing any horror one's imagination failed to conceive the utter dreadfulness of her position.

Perhaps she was mercifully unaware of the truth respecting her husband's mental state. I hoped so; but there was the frightful change in her appearance to be accounted for. It was just such a change as one might expect to find in a person who had been subjected to unspeakable nerve-racking experiences.

I determined to stay at Berner's Abbey until I should have laid bare its secret—or carried Leonora off to some place where she might receive the influences of healthy company and peaceful surroundings. Either course would be satisfactory, I thought; but I could not leave her here.

And, thinking that, I turned towards the wardrobe to see what it held in the way of clothing.

But in the act of reaching out to open the door I paused, staring at my hand. The hand was perfectly dry by this time, but in the lines of the palm and the finger joints were red wisps of blood. The rest of the hand was fairly clean. It was as though the rain had washed any blood that might have been there into the crevices, where it had congealed.

Nowhere about me was there a cut.

Then I remembered. It was my left hand; and it was in my left hand that I had held the glass container when St. Arnaud flew at me in that sudden burst of insane fury.

CHAPTER IV

THE EMERALD GREEN
MACKINTOSH

I AM USED TO THE SIGHT OF BLOOD, and by this time I thought that I had fully conquered the aversion that had reached its height when I started my hospital experience. And now, probably, it was not so much the physical presence of the blood as the suggestion behind it that affected me; but certain it is that I felt a kind of horror creeping over me.

Making an effort of the will, I tried to dismiss the horror; but do what I might I could not forget that shriek in the wood when the first crack of thunder broke just over the trees. And I found myself wondering what connection that shriek had with the blood on my hand.

And these thoughts reminded me in turn of the innumerable silent rooms lying all about me; and I could hear the beating of my own heart. And I said to myself: "You are afraid to open that wardrobe!" And it was true: I was afraid to open that wardrobe.

But not for long. When I found that my imagination was getting the upper hand of me and that I was reaching the stage where one feels that hidden eyes are watching one's back, I took a grip upon myself and, adopting a casual, almost swaggering air of indifference, I threw the door wide.

The wardrobe was a perfectly innocent affair. Had I allowed my imagination full play I should no doubt have likened the suits hanging there to a row of dead men; but with the most business-like air in the world I selected one—for St.

Arnaud and I were of a size—and then searched about for such other garments as I should require.

And then I went whistling to the bathroom, thinking of Piccadilly as I had seen it in the bright sunshine only that afternoon, and wondering how I could have been so easily driven into a state of "nerves".

And in due course, dryly clad in a dark-grey lounge suit, I took up the lamp and set off along the corridor towards the main staircase.

Far below in the hall there was a faint glow, presumably from the open door of the drawing-room, and I wondered whether Leonora had yet returned from her visit to St. Arnaud.

She had not. The room was just as we had left it. I set the lamp on the small table on which it had previously stood, and started to pace about the carpet. I must have waited there for the best part of an hour. The silence was more "positive" than any silence I had ever experienced. It was terrific. The storm had now ceased completely and there was no wind. Somewhere in the vast mansion were Leonora and St. Arnaud, but where I had no notion, and I might search half the night without discovering them. Therefore, I could only wait and try to keep the ghostly atmosphere from taking a hold on me.

I feared for Leonora. As the minutes went past and she did not return I began to form all sorts of conjectures to account for her long absence; and it is illustrative of the power of atmosphere that all my conjectures were of a disturbing—I might say horrible—kind.

Really, I was the man least fitted for the job I had set myself.

I was still pacing the carpet, keeping within the circle of light thrown by the lamps and acutely aware of the vague gloom at the other end of the apartment when I heard a swish-swish on the staircase. And there, at the door, stood Leonora.

"Come and help me, John," she said, and I could see that her fingers were twitching nervously and that her eyes were full of concern. "There's something wrong with Paul. Bring one of the lamps."

I hurried to her. She clutched at the sleeve of my coat and almost dragged me towards the staircase, and she kept a firm hold upon me all the way up, never saying a word but now and again making a sound that was something like an exclamation of impatience.

I asked her what was the matter with Paul, but she did not answer me; and so she hurried me up and up to the very highest gallery. Then, after threading a number of bewildering corridors, she opened a door by which the end of one corridor was blocked. I had only a glimpse of the room beyond this door, for, as I was about to follow her in, she suddenly turned on me with quite unreasonable fury and pushed me back into the corridor.

"You mustn't come in here!" she screamed. "No one wants you in here." And she looked at me for all the world as though she and I were the bitterest enemies.

She went into the room and partly closed the door behind her. But I had already had one glimpse of the room, and I knew it to be the laboratory. It was lighted by electricity, but the glass of the bulbs was of a greyish blue and the effect of this greyish blue light was singularly weird. All about the walls were marble shelves, holding the usual vessels and instruments to be found in laboratories, and in the middle of the floor stood a solidly-built table, seven or eight feet long and about three feet wide, whose top was a solid slab of marble.

It was this table that had claimed the most of my attention during my momentary survey of the apartment, for lying across it, his feet dragging on the floor and his head hanging down the other side, was St. Arnaud.

Then the door opened and I heard the sounds of physical exertion. And presently Leonora appeared, dragging the limp body of her husband across the floor. I wanted to help her, but I remained where I was; and not until she had dragged the body quite outside the room and had shut the door after switching off the lights, did I set the lamp down on a window sill and take an active interest in the matter.

St. Arnaud, I could see, was not quite unconscious though he was dazed; and after I had taken a good look at him I turned to Leonora, who had now laid the body flat on the floor and was gazing at it with an affrighted frown.

"We'll get him to bed," I said, "and get something hot into him. If you'll show me where to take him, I'll be able to manage while you get some hot water. And some brandy, if you have any. And is there a telephone here?"

She nodded her head.

"Well, telephone for a doctor first of all. I'm not a doctor yet, but I can do something to help in the meantime. He's still in his wet clothes. That's what's done it. I told him he ought to change at once, but he said—"

I did not pause to tell her what he had said, but bent down and raised St. Arnaud, and, under her directions, took him into a room close at hand where there was a bed and where a fire was laid in the grate.

And while I was half-dragging, half-carrying him along the corridor I remembered exactly what it was that he had said when I advised him to change immediately. He had spoken of being able to keep physical disorders at bay by the mere exercise of the will. And here be was, struck down into an inert mass by one of the most common of physical disorders!

I started to undress him. Leonora, meanwhile, had gone off to fulfill the various jobs I had mentioned, and I thought then that here was a good opportunity for me to slip along and take a more thorough look at that laboratory. I was sure that two minutes in there would give me some knowledge of the kind of investigations in which St. Arnaud was engaged. But my first duty was towards the man under my care and, though I confess that at the bottom of my heart I was not anxious to help him, I consciously did my utmost for his welfare.

"And if we can't save you," I said to his unresponsive figure as I tucked him up in the bed, "you'll have a first-rate opportunity for testing your theories. And by the looks of you," I added, "the job of saving you isn't going to be quite a straightforward affair."

I lighted the fire after some difficulty. The coals were covered with a layer of dust, showing that the fire had been laid for a very considerable time, and the paper and wood were damp and at first set up a thick while smoke; but soon the flames began to burn clearly. Then, after a glance around the room which had the appearance of being a servant's bed-room, I returned to the bed and looked down at the sick man.

Altogether, St. Arnaud was a man to inspire fear rather than love; and when one studied his features one could very readily credit him with the darkest of dealings and could believe that he had been serious when he spoke that blasphemy about the will being able to conquer death.

Leonora returned. She carried a large can of hot water in one hand and some glasses and bottles in a bowl in the other. These she put down without a word and walked straight towards the bed, where she stood staring down at her husband, her fingers twitching as before, her brow furrowed by lines of concern or of fear. Of me she took not the slightest notice.

For the next two or three minutes I was engaged in doing what I could for the sick man. Then I asked her, casually, whether she had telephoned for a doctor.

She did not answer, but continued to look down into the face of her husband. I repeated my question.

Still she did not answer. Then some movement of mine apparently attracted her attention, for she looked up at me with an expression of surprise as though she were only then aware of my presence.

"Oh, John! You don't think he'll die, do you?"

I noticed that her fists were clenched and that she was looking into my eyes in intense anticipation.

"I hope not," I said. "I see no reason why he should. Did you telephone for a doctor?"

"Yes. He said he would come at once. You're sure it's nothing serious? You see, he's never been ill. And if he were to die . . ."

Her whole mind was on her husband. She did not finish her last sentence, but, unfinished as it was, it conveyed the idea that no tragedy could be more appalling than the death of this man. And that struck me as very strange.

The distant sound of a bell came faintly through the dark wilderness of the mansion.

Leonora apparently did not hear it. She had returned to her position by the side of the bed and was staring down as before into the face of her husband.

I left the room and hurried off in the direction of the main staircase. The moon had now risen and was shining fitfully between the clouds which were being driven along by a wind that I could hear sighing in the trees outside. And the moonbeams, coming through the stained glass windows of the corridor in ghostly blue and red, helped me to find my way. The main staircase was lighted by a dome of ground glass, and the pale glow that came from this showed me the route round the several galleries and minor stairways. But I could not help thinking, with something of a shudder, that this was like spending a night in a museum.

I reached the hall and hurried to the front door, forming words of apology for having kept the doctor waiting so long. But I checked my course and, running into the drawing-room, snatched up the lamp that was still burning there.

When I opened the door, however, it was not the doctor who stood outside. It was a girl, whom I judged to be about eighteen. She was a remarkably beautiful girl—the fact I observed immediately—and she wore a mackintosh of a brilliant emerald green.

I murmured something, but instead of stating her business she stepped forward as though to walk right past me.

With as much tact as I could display I intercepted her. I was not going to be treated negligently, even by such a beautiful girl as this one was.

"Do you want to see Mrs. St. Arnaud?" I asked.

She stopped and looked at me rather blankly.

"The gentleman—" she said, and again made to pass me.

"Mr. St. Arnaud?" I questioned. "I'm afraid you can't see him to-night. He's ill. He's not conscious at the moment. It's impossible for him to have visitors."

She seemed to have difficulty in absorbing what I told her.

"He wants me," she said, and took a step forward as though for the stairs. She spoke with a curious lack of animation—a similar lack of animation to what I had observed in Leonora when I first saw her on that evening.

"I'm sorry," I told her, "but he can't see anybody. If you care to see Mrs. St. Arnaud . . . Or perhaps you would leave your name . . .?"

I was thoroughly puzzled by her manner. She was well-dressed and she spoke with a fairly cultured voice; but she did not display the politeness that one might expect from such a person. Her mind seemed to be obsessed with the single idea of seeing St. Arnaud. I was merely an obstacle in her path.

By now she had her hand raised as though to push me out of the way, and her face was showing irritable impatience.

"Look here!" I said. "You can't see Mr. St. Arnaud to-night. I tell you he's ill—unconscious. Can't have any visitors."

She stared at me as though trying to make out what I was driving at. In this moment of inactivity on her part I took the liberty of putting my hand on her arm and gradually turning her towards the door. To my surprise, she took the hint. Without a word she went slowly down the steps, and at the same slow pace, made off in the direction of the drive.

I stood watching her and wondering how I could fit her into the scheme of my observations on those associated with Berner's Abbey. I was sure that she was not in her normal state. She seemed to be dazed—in the same way as Leonora was sometimes dazed. It was strange, too, that she should call at this time of night. And it was still more strange that she should ask for "the gentleman," giving the impression that she did not even know St. Arnaud's name. Was she the woman whose scream I had heard in the wood? But it was useless to put such questions to myself. I was not yet in a position to answer questions. I could only make observations and wonder.

My reflections were cut short by the sudden flash of a car's headlights through the trees. And the last I saw of the girl—for that night, at least—was when the sweeping beams of light were reflected for an instant by her brilliant emerald green mackintosh.

"I'm Dr. Bonner," said a deep metallic voice as I went down the steps and opened the door of the car that had just drawn up.

CHAPTER V

THE END OF A VIGIL

LMOST MY FIRST WORDS to Dr. Bonner were words of apology for the shortcomings of the domestic arrangements.

Dr. Bonner, however was not surprised to learn that the domestic arrangements were almost non-existent. He was a medium-sized man of about fifty, and he had a penetrating eye. And it was when we had reached about the second gallery that he turned his penetrating eye upon me.

"I might say, Mr. Richmond," he remarked, "that I didn't expect to be met by a swarm of footmen. I've never seen Mr. St. Arnaud—though he bought this place about ten years ago—but I've heard more than a little about him. However—" There he broke off to say: "You're a doctor, aren't you?"

I told him that I was only a backward student.

"I thought you knew something about it," he went on. "Well, look here, Richmond! You want to get that cousin of yours to take a holiday. And a long holiday. Gather a few of your family together and make up a party for the West Indies or somewhere, leaving St. Arnaud at home. I saw Mrs. St. Arnaud about a month ago in the village, and I said to myself: 'You've got all sails set for the Golden Shore, my lady, or I never opened a text-book.' But, of course, you can see that for yourself, Richmond. Nerves gone to blazes! And you can't wonder at it. Living here, over two miles from your next-door neighbour—living in these catacombs without a soul about the place except St. Arnaud! And from what I can gather, he isn't exactly light-hearted company."

"Do you know anything about him, Doctor?" I asked eagerly. "I agree with you about my cousin, and when you see

her now you'll probably be even more emphatic in your
opinion. But do you know anything about St. Arnaud?"

"I know a lot," he replied, "if I care to believe all I hear.
But as I don't care to believe all I hear . . ."

"And what do you hear?" I asked, and added: "I might
say I'm prepared to believe almost anything about him."

He seemed disinclined to answer my question. He gave a
short laugh as though to say that it would be a waste of time
to talk about the matter. But I was persistent. I judged that
any scraps of local gossip would yield a certain amount of
truth. And it might require only a grain of truth to set me
along the right road of inquiry.

"Well, for one thing," said Dr. Bonner, "they say he's
mad. But they would say that of anybody who shut himself
up with a lot of retorts and test-tubes . . . What an uncanny
mausoleum of a place this is!"

"What else do they say?" I persisted.

"They say—the more intellectual of them—that he deals
in Indian magic. You would be surprised at the number of
otherwise level-headed people who believe in magic.
They've got other names for it, of course, but they mean
magic all the same. And because a fellow with a turban on
his head came here about six months ago they jump to the
conclusion that it's Indian magic."

He stopped for breath and looked over the balustrade of
the gallery on which we happened to be standing.

"That moonlight shining through those windows," he
said, pointing to one of the lower corridors, "is enough to
send anybody mad. What a mausoleum!" he repeated.

We moved forward.

"And some say," he went on, returning to the subject of
St. Arnaud, "that's he's looking for perpetual motion, and
some say he's looking for the 'elixir vitae.' But you can
imagine for yourself just what they do say."

We were now at the door of the chamber in which St. Arnaud lay. We had lost ourselves once on the way up, and
though I was eager to hear anything that Dr. Bonner had to
tell me, I could not very well delay our arrival any longer.

Leonora was still standing in the same position, looking down on the face of her husband with the same intense expression of concern. She did not move even when we entered and I saw the doctor looking at her with narrowed eyes. For the first few moments, in fact, he seemed to be more interested in Leonora than in the patient.

Then, after a fairly exhaustive examination of St. Arnaud who was now breathing quickly and with apparent difficulty, he drew me aside. I had received the impression that Dr. Bonner was a man who would remain calm in any circumstances, but I could see that he was agitated as a result of his examination of St. Arnaud.

"Now, look here, Richmond," he said in a markedly severe tone, "I'm not satisfied with your management of this case. You haven't managed it. You've made a mess of it. You had no right to undertake it. You ought to have sent for me a couple of days ago."

I looked at him in amazement.

"You're only a student, you must remember," he went on. "You certainly had no right to undertake such a case as this."

"But he was only taken bad to-night," I said, resenting his words, but knowing that they would be justified if they were true. "He was only taken bad about two hours ago. And I only arrived here to-night. We were both caught in that thunderstorm."

He looked at me as though I were speaking gibberish.

"But he couldn't have been out to-night," he said. "The thing would be impossible."

"But he was out to-night," I persisted, "I met him—out in the grounds as I was walking over from the station. The two of us ran most of the way home here in the rain."

"He ran!"

"Yes. Part of the way up the hill, too. I thought it was the soaking he got that had knocked him over."

The doctor looked first at me and then at the man on the bed.

"Well, I should have said that he was due to be knocked over two or three days ago. Excuse me, Richmond, for speaking as I did; but I should never have believed that a man in his state could walk about."

There was no doubt that he was utterly puzzled. But he shrugged his shoulders with an air of a man who is accepting the inevitable, and returned to the patient. And for another half an hour he busied himself with making the best of a bad affair, and I had my time fully occupied in fetching and carrying for him. On one occasion I had to find my way to the kitchen, for we could obtain no help whatsoever from Leonora, who simply stood gazing down at St. Arnaud and who seemed unable to understand what we were about.

St. Arnaud's case was a puzzle to Dr. Bonner. But to me it was more than a puzzle; it had a tremendous significance that brought it into line with all the other strange matters that I had observed during my few hours at Berner's Abbey,

Dr. Bonner merely wondered how a man in an advanced stage of pneumonia could have the strength to run about the countryside. And I might have been more settled in my mind had I known no more than Dr. Bonner knew. But St. Arnaud himself had told me that he believed that the power of the will could conquer physical ailments, and now there could be no doubt that to a remarkable extent he had been right.

For two or three days his will had kept him at the top of his strength while he had been suffering from a disease that would have prostrated any other man whatsoever. I honestly believe that if it had not been for the tremendous extra handicap of the drenching in the rain and the supervening chill, he would have recovered from the attack of pneumonia while still on his feet and without turning a hair. And I make that statement knowing perfectly well the history of pneumonia and knowing that a man of St. Arnaud's age is in the gravest danger from the disease, even with the most careful medical attention.

But it had now conquered him so far as carrying him off his feet went. I could see that Dr. Bonner was regarding the case with the utmost seriousness. And now that I knew how ill the man was, I too began to take a really serious view of the case.

She herself did not seem to be aware of the truth, and what puzzled me most of all was her present stunned condition—a condition suggesting that she would consider his death as the supreme tragedy of her existence. But I knew that she would recover from his death and that her life would henceforth be happier than it had been.

In due course Dr. Bonner went. He had spoken about nurses, but I had told him that I could do all the nursing that was required; and after being given minute instructions for the care of the patient during the night, I accompanied the doctor to the door. He said he would go home and snatch a few hours' sleep and call back again early in the morning.

And so, lamp in hand, I returned into the silent mausoleum of a mansion whose only other occupants were a woman who merely existed in a dazed condition and a dying man.

I had now no doubt that St. Arnaud was dying. His much-vaunted will was in abeyance and he could not now arrest the progress of the disease.

Yet, as I took my silent way up the great staircase, I could not help having an uncomfortable sensation down the spine when I thought of the conviction with which he had spoken of being able to defeat death itself.

In that silent place anything might be possible, and I was ready to share with the more superstitious of the surrounding country folk the belief that St. Arnaud was a wizard.

Leonora was still standing where I had left her.

She had not paid the slightest heed to the doctor and me. I doubt whether she knew that the doctor had been.

I spoke to her—asked her whether she wouldn't sit down; but she did not hear me. I touched her, to call her attention to a chair I had just placed by the bedside for her; but even that did not disturb the intensity her gaze at the face of the man lying on the bed.

Hour after hour she stood there, her lips moving in prayer, her gaze never wavering for an instant.

I was amazed at her powers of endurance. But chiefly I was horrified at the unholy significance of the spectacle. I could not scoff at it. I could not regard it as being other than profoundly serious. I looked on in fear and awe, and with every passing moment I expected to see some manifestation of the power that she was invoking.

The hours passed with incredible slowness. Now and again I was engaged in attending to the patient, though as the night wore on I could see that he would soon be beyond my assistance, and at these times I was able to forget Leonora. But whenever I took up my position again at the foot of the bed I could not escape the singularly horrifying effect of her silent presence.

It was still an hour or two before sunrise. From my last examination of St. Arnaud I knew that the end might occur at any moment. I wondered what would happen then. Even with my mediocre medical knowledge, though it was backed, of course, by a consultation with Dr. Bonner, I was convinced that no power could save his life.

Yet, as I watched Leonora—whose white, emaciated face threw into prominence her half-closed eyes that now glowed darkly with intense expression—as I watched Leonora I believed in the impossible, and I half expected to see the man rise up in the very moment of death.

I had done all I could. I was waiting now for the end. And I did not dare to imagine what manifestation of hidden power the end might bring.

A startled exclamation from Leonora awoke me from a spell of abstraction into which I had fallen. I rushed round to the side of the bed. One glance at the face of St. Arnaud was enough to tell me that he had passed away.

The feeling of horror left me immediately. He was dead, and nothing had happened. Already the process of dissolution had started, and no power could recall the spirit which might animate this dead body.

But I examined him thoroughly. And during the examination I chanced to glance up at Leonora.

She was looking on in the uncomprehending way that I had observed in moments of our talk when I first arrived. The intense express had gone from her face.

I wondered at this sudden calmness. After a whole night's earnest concentration for the purpose—so I assumed —of defeating death, it was to be expected that she should show a corresponding excess of disappointment at the failure of her efforts. But she merely looked about the room in the most casual manner imaginable.

Then I remembered the urgency with which she had begged me to try to save him, and I wondered afresh that she should now take his death so calmly, that she should not be prostrated with grief.

She put her hands to her eyes and rubbed them, giving the impression that she was just awaking from sleep. In the meantime I had done all that was necessary with the dead body—had closed the eyes more firmly and had bound up the sagging jaw—and I was in the act of covering the face and head with the bed-sheet. In the midst of this rite Leonora seemed to spring suddenly to full consciousness.

"John!" she exclaimed, and the expression in her eyes as they sought and held mine was an expression of demoniacal joy. "Is he dead? Dead? Is it true that he's dead?"

Then with a wild nervous laugh she tore the sheet back from the dead face and, before I could rush round to stop her, had taken the shoulders in a grip that made her knuckles stand out whiter even than the prevailing whiteness of her hands.

I do not know what she intended to do. But judging by her manner, it was something harmful. I managed to pull her away, though in the struggle she dragged the body almost into a sitting position, from which it fell back and rested ungracefully with its head twisted sideways.

It required all my strength to overcome her. She fought like a wild beast and continually strove to reach the corpse. I assumed that she had completely lost her reason, and while that somewhat modified the horror of sacrilege, it filled me with a different and more personal horror.

All this time she had been half crying and half laughing in a torrent of insane whines and murmurings; but now she found her voice.

"You devil!" she cried, addressing the corpse. "You fiend! You fiend of darkness! Now your soul's gone to Satan. And your body ought to be—"

I put my hand over her mouth to stop the flow of vituperation. I took my hand from her mouth and released her. She turned and buried her head on my shoulder and started to cry.

"Forgive me, John!" she sobbed. "You must have thought me mad. Sometimes I have thought myself mad. But I'm not, John. It's he who was mad. He was worse than mad. I'll tell you about him. To-morrow. I'm too tired now. I feel exhausted. But what I said was true. He is a devil—a magician."

She turned her head and glanced at the corpse.

"He said he would never die," she murmured. Then she turned again to me. "But he really is dead, isn't he?"

I assured her that there was no doubt about that, and her answer was to give way to a more violent spasm of crying and to clutch me the tighter. I knew her tears to be the expression of relief, and that she was now experiencing the first health-giving emotion that had come her way in months perhaps. I let her sob, and some time later I took her downstairs.

Before leaving the bedroom I put the corpse into a more natural position, for I dreaded the thought of having to come up here alone later in order to perform that grisly duty.

In the drawing-room, with the first eerie greyness of the dawn coming through the windows, Leonora lay down on a couch and almost immediately fell asleep.

And I, with unspeakable gladness in my heart, watched over her.

When she awoke she would tell me her story, tell me all that had brought her to the very edge of insanity. And though I was impatient to hear that, I was mainly concerned with the joy of reflecting that her dreadful experiences were now ended and that the future would hold only happiness.

"He said he would never die, did he?" I ruminated.

And I smiled a superior smile.

CHAPTER VI

A WAVE OF FEAR

LEONORA SLEPT THE SLEEP OF UTTER EXHAUSTION. I was not surprised at this, remembering the strange nature of her vigil through the long hours of the night; and I was contented simply to watch her, knowing that she would awake refreshed and in a more suitable frame of mind for telling me the truth about St. Arnaud.

For, of course, I was eager to hear the story. Leonora's behaviour had been so contradictory that I was perfectly mystified by it, and by no speculation could I arrange the whole into a clear system. She had clung to St. Arnaud and yet she had hated him. She had shown frenzied joy at his death and yet she had begged me to save him. And she had said that he was a devil—a magician. Of that I took little enough notice.

She had spoken the words seriously, but at the time she had been distraught, and I guessed that when she awoke in a more peaceful state of mind she would modify these wild assertions.

The sun had now risen and, leaving Leonora, I found my way to the kitchens and commenced hunting about for something to eat. But finding something to eat was not such a simple matter as I expected it to be, for the kitchens and larders had been built to minister to the wants of a regiment of people. But at last I discovered the corner where the food was kept, and selected a couple of eggs and found bread and butter and tea.

Fortunately the fire, which I had replenished last night when I was running about at Dr. Bonner's orders, was still glowing redly; and in a very few minutes I was seated at a deal table eating boiled eggs and thick slices of bread and butter. I reflected that I must learn to be somewhat daintier when cutting bread. But I thoroughly enjoyed the meal, even though the eggs would have been the better for a few minutes' more boiling; and I thought that one day Leonora and I might laugh over my attempt at preparing a meal suitable for a hungry man.

As I wandered out about the gravel I was struck by the ideal situation of Berner's Abbey, and in the brightness that was everywhere around me I found it hard to believe that last night had held such terrors.

I could not go far from the front of the place, for I did not know when Dr. Bonner might pay his promised visit; but my strolling took me round to the oldest part of the mansion. In point of fact, I was trying to see whether I could locate the electric lighting plant, for I intended to have a look at it to see whether I could get it into going order before nightfall. But all the outhouses at the back were locked, so I wandered round towards the front again, stopping on the way to examine the West Tower which is the original part of Berner's Abbey and which was probably a real abbey at one time.

My thoughts, as I say, were perfectly pleasant, and as my gaze travelled upwards over the surface of the grey stones, right to the battlements at the top, I was merely speculating on how much had happened in the world since these stones were first placed in their present position.

Then suddenly I became uneasy. Remembering my journeys to and fro between the hall and the sick room last night, I judged that I was looking at that part of the building in which the dead body of St. Arnaud lay. Why that should cause me to feel uneasy I could not tell, for plain reason told me that it was only a corpse that lay up there and that the mysterious activities of St. Arnaud were finished for ever.

But I could not shake off the feeling, and there would persist in coming to my mind Leonora's words: "He said he would never die." I turned away, feeling foolish for having entertained any fears whatsoever. The man was dead. Without a doubt he was dead. When I had laid the body in a natural position, just before escorting Leonora downstairs, rigor mortis had already begun to set in. I had seen too many dead bodies in my short experience to have any doubt about the death of St. Arnaud; and in any case, I should soon have Dr. Bonner here to give the certificate.

I was now looking down towards a walled-in part of the grounds at some distance from the house. It lay amidst trees, for trees were all about the mansion which had been built in a clearing on this high ridge of land. In one corner of the walled-in part there was a tiny chapel. I had not paid much attention to this feature of the grounds during my previous one or two visits to Berner's Abbey, but now I recognized it as the burial ground of the families who had owned the place in the past.

This recalled me to the business that would have to be done during the next day or two. Unless St. Arnaud had relatives within easy call—and I had never heard of his having any relatives whatsoever—I presumed that the business of the funeral would fall upon me. Naturally, I would make that my business for Leonora's sake. And I further reflected that it would be as well for me to telegraph immediately for my sister and her husband, Tommy Gallagher, to come down that day. It would hardly do for Leonora and me to stay in the place alone even in the present unusual circumstances. And I must get hold of a servant or two to look after things until the funeral was over. I did not expect that we would want anybody after that, for I guessed that Leonora would be only too ready to get away from Berner's Abbey.

The sound of a motor engine attracted my attention and I hurried round to the main doorway to meet Dr. Bonner, who was then just coming over the crest of the drive.

When I told him that St. Arnaud was dead, the doctor shrugged his shoulders and said that he wasn't surprised to hear it.

"How is Mrs. St. Arnaud?" he asked. "That's more important."

I told him that she was resting, that he might see her if he wished, for she was only lying on a couch in the drawing-room.

"Right," he said. "I'll have a look at her first."

Leonora was still asleep when we went into the drawing-room. Dr. Bonner went across and, standing over her, looked down into her face. It seemed to me that he stood there for a long time looking down into her face.

Then he turned to me.

"There's a change in her already," he said. "She's a very different person from the one I saw last night. Extraordinary! But let her sleep. She'll probably sleep half the day. Don't disturb her. And when this is all over, you see about getting her away for a long sea voyage. And when she comes back get her to take up golf."

The doctor's remarks on the sudden change for the better in Leonora's appearance suggested to me the notion of telling him just what had happened last night and in the early hours of this morning. I felt that I ought to tell him, seeing that he was taking so much interest in her. But I decided to wait until I had heard Leonora's full story from her own lips; and remembering all the strange things I had heard and witnessed, I thought it best to keep my own counsel in the meantime.

Perhaps the whole gruesome affair of the wizard of Berner's Abbey would have been more quickly settled had I told Dr. Bonner, there and then, all I knew. I think so now; but at the time I had no expectation of tragedy, for the man from whom tragedy might be looked for lay dead up near the top of the West Tower. And I did not want to draw unnecessary attention to Leonora. I had already settled my plans for the future, and these plans concerned only Leonora and me.

I conducted Dr. Bonner on the interminable journey to the death chamber. Even in the light of day the vast well of the staircase, with its galleries high one above the other, gave one a sense of the uncanny, and I was not sorry to think that my sister and Tommy Gallagher would be with us some time during the day. Tommy Gallagher, I might mention is one of the most typical he-men I have ever met—just the man to drive the uncanny atmosphere from a vault, if necessary—and that fact gave me a sense of relief.

In the natural light of day the corpse presented a singularly fearsome appearance. The hair and the moustache were an intense black, and the face had the whiteness of chalk. The face, in fact, seemed to have the physical properties of chalk, and with the hollow jaws and the high cheek-bones, the whole effect was such that I was glad that Dr. Bonner did not ask me to assist him in the examination. While he was engaged in this work I wandered over to the window and looked out, ready to pull down the blind whenever he should be finished.

The examination did not take long. It was over in a matter of minutes, I silently pulled down the blind and hurried after the doctor, who had gone out into the corridor.

I have previously said that I am no dare-devil; yet I ought not to have been afraid of a dead body, for I had seen dozens of dead bodies. But at that moment I was overtaken by a sudden access of fear. Leonora's unrestrained vituperation; her wild statements about St. Arnaud's being a devil—a magician; and his own assertion that he would never die—all these came back to me in that moment, and for the space of an instant I verily believed that the corpse might make some movement before I could reach the door.

A moment afterwards, I was walking along the corridor by the side of Dr. Bonner. I was thinking that my nervous system must be painfully out of order, and was contemplating taking up golf.

Yet, I have since had reason to believe that my nervous system was quite sound at that time, and I have also had reason to suspect that the wave of fear that overtook me during the moment in which I was in the room alone with the body of St. Arnaud had its cause in something.

Leonora was still asleep when we returned to the hall. The doctor gave me the death certificate. I explained to him that I wanted to go down to the village to see about the funeral arrangements and to send off a telegram. I also told him that I wanted to engage one or two temporary domestics, but that I could not leave Leonora alone in the place.

He solved all my difficulties at once. He said that he would call in at one of the cottages when he got to the village and send up an elderly couple who had formerly been on the staff of Berner's Abbey and that he would also ask the local undertaker to call. As for the telegram he reminded me that I could telephone that to the post office.

CHAPTER VII

LEONORA'S STORY

B Y THE TIME LEONORA AWOKE—about three o'clock in the afternoon—I had done all that I could towards making life bearable for the next few days, and had set in motion the machinery for performing the last rites over the mortal remains of St. Arnaud.

The undertaker had been and had gone. Tommy Gallagher had telephoned to say that he and Jane, my sister, would arrive during the early evening. I had had quite a cheery chat over the telephone with Tommy, and after I had explained the circumstances of the case as fully as I thought desirable, he said that he would regard the stay as a portion of his holiday. He gave the impression that, funeral or no funeral, he was looking forward to enjoying himself.

Then the elderly couple who were going to see to our physical comfort put in an appearance. They were, as Dr. Bonner had told me former servants of the place, and therefore they did not need any introduction to the domestic quarters.

I asked the man whether he had been employed in Berner's Abbey during Mr. St. Arnaud's time, and he answered yes, that he had been there up to a month ago. Then, on my asking why he had left the service of Mr. St. Arnaud, not he but his wife took it upon herself to reply, and I learnt from her that they had been the last of all the servants to go, and that they had gone for the same reason as all the others—namely, the queer behaviour of St. Arnaud.

"And what was queer about Mr. St. Arnaud's behaviour?" I asked, addressing the question to the man.

But it was the woman who answered. In fact, during all my dealings with this couple, it was the woman who conducted their side of the business. The man was of the naturally silent type and spoke only when there was no wriggling out of speech.

I hoped to learn something from Mrs. Groom—for Groom was the name of the couple—but she could only give a confused account of hearing noises during the nights. When I asked her what kind of noises, she hinted at the noise of people walking about in the corridors.

It was apparent that of her own experience she was aware of nothing definitely unusual. She said, however, that one of the other servants—a Welshman—had come upon St. Arnaud one night creeping stealthily behind Mrs. St. Arnaud as she was going upstairs and that Mrs. St. Arnaud, happening to turn and see her husband, had given a shriek of terror and had fled into the nearest room, locking the door. But that was only a story at secondhand and, whether true or not, did not help me a great deal.

"Was Mr. St. Arnaud a good master?" I asked. "I mean, in the way of wages and the amount of work he expected you to do, and so on."

Mrs. Groom said that he was. He paid excellent wages and, so far as the work was concerned, the servants could do pretty much as they pleased.

That being so, I told myself, there must have been something in the stories of the local gossips referred to by Dr. Bonner, for servants don't as a rule leave a place that has the advantages of good wages and go-as-you-please duties.

"We was the last to go," said Mrs. Groom, "because we lived local. But when the rest left we couldn't stick it no longer. It was the loneliness and the queerness of the place; though we hated to leave Mrs. St. Arnaud, and that's a fact. And we wouldn't have come back for no money in the world only that that man's dead. He used to fair give me the creeps. We never knew what might happen next, if you understand what I mean."

I did understand what she meant. I, too, had had experience of the queerness of the place, and I guessed that it was nothing more definite than the ghostly atmosphere of the house that had driven them away.

So Mr. and Mrs. Groom settled themselves in without any delay, and justified the high wages I had offered on behalf of Leonora by providing me with a first-rate lunch.

Only in one matter did affairs refuse to run smoothly. The electric lighting plant could not be induced to function. I had only a layman's knowledge of dynamos, and Groom had no knowledge whatsoever, regarding a dynamo as a machine mysterious and more than human. And though we succeeded in getting the engine to go, we could not awake the faintest spark in the brushes of the dynamo. I decided to wait until Tommy Gallagher arrived. Tommy Gallagher knew about most things, and I had no doubt that a single glance at the switchboard would show him that I had failed to perform some essential act.

And now, here I was, sitting at a small tea-table in the drawing-room with Leonora sitting opposite me.

I had been present when she awoke. At one moment she had been soundly asleep, and when I looked at her a moment later she was lying gazing at me out of wide-open eyes. When I spoke to her she jumped up and looked about the room in an uncomprehending manner, then she appeared to recollect herself.

"He's dead!" she murmured and her face lit up with an expression of indescribable relief, and for the first time since my arrival she smiled a really natural smile.

I had no doubt that in a few days she would be her old self again.

I handed her over to the care of Mrs. Groom, whom she was surprised and delighted to see, and when she had gone to change I wandered about he drawing-room, happier than I had ever been in my life, going over in my mind the plans I had made for our immediate future.

These plans, needless to say, embraced our marriage at the earliest possible moment compatible with the usages of society. For myself, I had no delicate feelings about St. Arnaud's death. I would have married Leonora within a month and would not have been worried by thoughts of the respect due to her dead husband, but one had to be careful not to offend the susceptibilities of the world.

But there was no need to be impatient. I knew that we should be married all in good time. Of course, I had not mentioned that matter to Leonora, but I was perfectly well aware, by a hundred minute signs, that her affection for me was as much alive now as it had ever been. Therefore, as I say, I was in the pleasantest spirits as I waited for her to join me over the tea-table. And, as I say, I was not aware of being guilty of any disrespect towards the memory of her late husband.

"You know," she said, while he was pouring out the tea, "I can hardly believe its true. It seems—" She hesitated, searching for a suitable expression. "It seems too wonderful!"

In ordinary circumstances, such a remark might be regarded as that of person utterly without decency. But Leonora made it. And she made it to the accompaniment of a smile of such innocent happiness that it was robbed of all its offensiveness. It was the sincere expression of relief of one who had returned to life after a sojourn among the unspeakable tortures of outer darkness.

"Don't tell me about it now, if you would rather not," I said. "It would be very much wiser if, for the next few days, you would try to forget all about it—or, at least, think as little about it as possible. Jane and Tommy Gallagher will be down this evening. They'll give you something else to think about."

"But I want—"

"And when it's all over, you must go away for a long holiday," I continued. "Dr. Bonner says a voyage to the West Indies in cheerful company. He also recommends golf—eighteen holes in the morning and eighteen holes the afternoon. That will be when you come back, for they don't have eighteen-hole golf courses on board ship."

"But listen a minute, John," she said. "I want to tell you about it. I must tell you about it. I must tell someone. When I have told someone I'll feel that I can go ahead with this 'cure' that Dr. Bonner prescribes."

"I understand," I replied; and added as lightly as I could, judging it best to create as happy an atmosphere as possible: "Go ahead! But don't forget that I'll want another cup of tea in about a couple of shakes."

She refused to respond to the lightness of my assumed mood.

"You have heard the expression, 'a living death'?" she asked, and went on. "That's regarded as a metaphor; one could never conceive a living death. But I have conceived it. I have experienced it."

She paused and looked into the distance.

As for me, the assumed lightness had simply left me. There was nothing consciously dramatic in her manner, but her plain sincerity was more powerful than the most finely calculated effect.

"You remember when I first met him," she continued. "You and I were just on the point of becoming engaged to be married, and I broke the engagement off. I forget what I said. There are many things I do forget . . . At moments since—for I have had moments of sanity—I have wondered what you thought of me. But I couldn't help it. I mean that literally—I had no choice; I simply couldn't help it."

"You mean," I interrupted, "that you had something more than a material inducement to desert me and marry him?"

"It went beyond all material things," she replied. "I have heard of people marrying against their inclinations in order that some greater good might be achieved—turning them-selves into martyrs for various reasons, family reasons and so on. But there was nothing of that sort in my case. I simply had no choice. He asked me to marry him and I said yes. I couldn't say no. He dominated me in some curious way. I just had to do as he wanted me to do.

"Yet, I disliked him from the first. When I realized what I had done I was intensely unhappy—over you and the collapse of our dream. But gradually I began to forget you. I could not make out what had come over me. I did not seem to be the same person as I had been. I don't know whether you understand, but I'm afraid I can't put it any clearer. I seemed to lose my identity. I found myself thinking thoughts and doing acts that were quite opposed to my former character. Do you follow me?"

I was trying hard to gain a notion of her mental state, but she must have noticed the puzzled expression on my face, for she went on:

"Once, for instance, when he had gone to London and I was left here, I went up to the laboratory and started measuring out chemicals. I had been on the point of going to bed, for he had said that he wouldn't be home until the next day; but instead of going to bed I went up to the laboratory. I don't know why I went; I just went. And I was there all night, measuring out chemicals and making notes in a book. And I don't know anything whatever about chemistry. Yet I kept on all through the night, mixing up one lot of chemicals and making a note of the result, then throwing the mixture down the sink because it wasn't right, then beginning all over again. And I didn't know what I was trying to do, yet I felt that I had to keep on. At last I seemed to know that I had got it right—whatever it was—and I came downstairs and went to bed.

"When I woke up the next day I thought I had been dreaming, so I went to the laboratory again to look at the book. He was there, and he patted me on the back and told me that I had been successful. He was looking over the signs and things I had put in the book.

"It was then that I began to know what fear was. I suspected the truth then. Whether he had hypnotized me or not I don't know; but I do know that I was existing under his will and not under my own. We were two distinct persons physically, but so far as our mental life went we were only one. John, can you imagine the horror of that? I had no will. I had no thoughts of my own, and yet I was I. I had all the agony of knowing my position, but I hadn't the power to do a single thing to alter it.

"I'm afraid you can't appreciate what that means. You can't know the value of a free will until it is taken from you, and only then can you know the horror of having a moral sense and yet not having the power to act according to that moral sense.

"You know what nightmare is? You know that feeling of being present somewhere and of wanting to prevent something from happening, and yet being unable to move? And you know that sense of terror that you get. You feel that you are surrounded by sinister things; every object takes on a horribly sinister identity. This was like that; but it was worse, because I knew I wasn't dreaming. I knew I was awake and going about among other people, but I had the sense of being isolated from the everyday world.

"Have you ever thought what it might be like if you were to die and to find yourself out in the void—alone in a strange blackness; only you—and eternity? That's how I felt. I had lost touch with things familiar . . . Oh, I can't explain! It was simply an existence of terror.

"I learnt what my husband was doing—what his work was. He was trying to discover the spirit that animates living things. He was mad—though I don't know. Yet I thought he was mad, and that added to my horror, for I knew that my mind was existing with his—was merged into his—and I knew that I should be forced to go through whatever terrors his insane fancy conceived.

"He made me his accomplice in his blasphemous work," she went on. She was greatly agitated now, and her eyes were shining with the intensity of her feelings. "He said that he could will dead things to live. He said that the will existed apart from the body—or something like that. At that time I seemed to be convinced that he was right; but now that he is dead all my comprehension of that sort of thing has gone.

"I had a dog once, and one day I took him up to the laboratory and killed him—stabbed him with a sheath-knife—and then—But I needn't tell you all the abominations that

have taken place in that laboratory. But some day I might—
must. I must share the memory of them with someone for the
sake of feeling that they aren't hidden away in my own mind.
And I don't remember everything. There are gaps in my existence that probably hide worse things than I know. Once I
suddenly returned to consciousness and found that I was
standing outside the door of one of the servant's rooms, and I
had that sheath-knife in my hand. He was in London at the
time. If he had been in the house I should have killed him.
But, of course, I couldn't have killed him. Sometimes I
found myself able to act according to my own judgment; he
would let me go free for a time now and again. When I came
to normal consciousness outside the servant's bedroom—that
was one of the times when I felt myself to be free. But of
course I couldn't have killed him. Had I tried to I should
immediately have found myself in the nightmare state—
utterly without the power to act of my own will.

"I have gone for a week without sleep when he wanted
me to help him. It was his will and my body. I just had to
keep going. Physically I would feel dead—so thoroughly exhausted that I could have sold my soul to be able to drop
down and go to sleep—but I hadn't the will to stop doing
whatever it was that he had set me to do. Something like that
happened last night, but it wasn't for long. It ended abruptly
when he died. But it might have gone on for days. Were you
there when he made me stand by his bed and try to keep him
alive?"

I nodded. The case was clearer to me now. St. Arnaud,
with his mad obsession about the power of the will, had
brought his own will to a remarkable state of efficiency. It
had been a simple matter for him to hypnotize Leonora and
to keep her completely under his dominion. I moved my
chair to the other side of the table and took her hand in mine.
She was right when she said that I would find it almost impossible to conceive the horrors through which she had gone.
Yet I was appalled by the mere contemplation of the fearful
possibilities that lay behind her story. The wonder was that
she hadn't gone completely insane.

"Don't worry," I said, feeling that the words were childishly inadequate, for I knew that the horror would stay with her for a long time and that her complete recovery would be a delicate business. And, realizing the inadequacy of the injunction not to worry, I added: "Try not to think of it all as having actually happened."

"But I can't do that," she said. "I know it did happen, and I haven't told you a tenth part—not a thousandth part—of all that happened. I've merely tried to show you the kind of thing that was happening. I could tell you things that would make your blood run cold—physical things. That man was a monster. He was utterly inhuman. He had one fixed idea—that of bringing dead animal tissue back to life—and nothing else was of any consequence to him. Forgive me, John, for speaking about such horrible things. I don't want to disgust you, but I must tell someone.

"The physical side of it all used to sicken me at first," she went on, "but after a time I became accustomed to it. It was the other side that never lost its horror—the spiritual side. The thought of being physically alive and yet being spiritually dead was terrible. My spirit seemed to be wandering about in a void—chaos. Now and again I got a glimpse of normal things. I would realize suddenly that I was talking to one of the servants, for instance, but it would all seem unreal. That night that you arrived—"

"Last night?" I said.

"Was that only last night? It seems ages ago. Anyway, I found myself speaking to you out in the rain. I have no recollection of going out in the rain."

I thought it better not to make any observations now on the strangeness of her manner on that occasion. St. Arnaud, when he dropped that glass container, had wished her to come and help to find it. And she had come. That incident, now that I understood it, helped me to get some idea of the terrible plight that Leonora had been in.

"But he's dead now," I said, judging that she had disburdened her mind sufficiently for the time being, and wishing to lead her to the contemplation of happier things. "You've only to think about getting better. Tommy and Jane will be here very shortly now; they'll give you brighter things to think about. It's only a matter of time before you find yourself the same person as you used to be. You know that he can't harm you now."

She did not answer immediately. She rose from the table and I followed suit. It was then that I noticed that neither of us had eaten anything and that a creamy surface had formed on our cold untasted tea.

"He said he would never die," she murmured. "But he is dead, isn't he?"

"Of course he's dead," I said lightly, scornfully, disrespectfully, as I took her through the hall and out into the afternoon sunshine. "Let's have a blow of fresh air."

CHAPTER VIII

NEWS FROM THE VALLEY

FOR AN HOUR OR SO Leonora and I sauntered about the grounds. I kept the conversation along general lines, telling her what I had been doing lately and discussing recent events in the wider world.

I had to refer, of course, to the business of the funeral. I told Leonora what I had done, and asked whether there were any friends on either side who ought to be informed of the death.

She said no. For her part she had no very close relatives, and such relatives as she had could be told of the death by letter—sometime. She was perfectly apathetic in that matter. And she knew of no one related to St. Arnaud. She understood that he was French, though she was not sure even about that. His antecedents were wrapped in mystery. He had come to her out of the unknown emblematic of his whole character, and she would not trouble now to make inquiries about him.

"You say you have arranged to have him buried in the private burial ground?" she asked.

"Yes," I told her. "The undertaker suggested it. I agreed. I never gave it a thought. Perhaps you would rather—"

"Oh, I don't mind!" she said. "I shan't ever live here again. I shall have no further interest in the place."

"You'll sell it, I suppose?"

"No," she said "I shan't do anything with it. I suppose it's mine—I don't know. But I shan't accept it. I shan't accept anything that ever belonged to him. I'll stay here until he's buried, but I'll leave the place immediately afterwards—

leave it just as it stands—and the authorities can do with it what they like. So he might as well be buried here as anywhere else. I'm perfectly indifferent."

It was while we were walking in the drive that Tommy Gallagher and my sister Jane arrived. I had telephoned for a car to meet them at the station, and here was the car coming at low gear up over the brow of the hill with Tommy's head and shoulders leaning out at one side.

He was in a sports suit. I had told him that no mourning would be worn, and I was not surprised at the sports suit. When the car stopped abreast of us and they got out walk the rest of the way with us, leaving the car to go forward alone with the luggage, I expected to see a bag of golf clubs in the interior; but apparently Tommy had realized that a funeral is a funeral after all, and had left his clubs behind. Or, more probably, Jane had argued him out of the golf clubs.

Jane kissed me, standing on her tiptoes. She is six years older than I but she's a little slip of a thing. Tommy, on the other hand, is huge—a man of about forty—and I saw Leonora wince when he shook hands with her. I winced too, although I thought I was ready for him.

He murmured some words of sympathy with Leonora, and Leonora replied very seriously. I took my cue from her and made up my mind to say nothing to either Tommy or Jane about the actual facts relating to St. Arnaud.

Tommy's spirits were momentarily damped. I had hinted to him on the telephone that the death was not the occasion for any real grief, and I could imagine that he would use that statement for all it was in his argument with Jane in the matter of the golf clubs—for I was positive that he had not left them behind from his own judgment on what was "done" and what was not "done".

He and I had fallen a pace or two behind Leonora and Jane.

"By the way," he said, "he wasn't murdered, was he? The—er—old boy, I mean."

I looked up at him.

"No," I said. "Why do you ask that? He died of pneumonia."

"Well, somebody's been murdered round about here, Jane!" he called and his shout could be heard up at the house, although Jane and Leonora were only a few yards ahead of us. "Did you hear who it was who—" He recollected himself and, waiting until we came up with the two women he said in a lower voice: "What was that fellow saying about somebody being found murdered? That fellow at the station. Did you hear him? He was telling that other chap—the one with the side-whiskers—about it."

"No," said Jane. "I remember the two men. Is that what they were talking about?"

"Sure. Somebody's head knocked in."

"Tommy! Please!" Jane exclaimed.

"Sorry!" said Tommy. "I just wondered whether you happened to overhear them."

We fell back a pace or two again.

He went on to talk about a man he knew who was going out to Canada with a new idea for felling timber or transporting timber or something of the sort. I was not listening. My mind was on his vague story about a murder in the neighbourhood.

One reads of plenty of murders, but the murders about which one reads have something impersonal about them. But I had the horribly disquieting feeling that this murder concerned me. There were many chances against it, of course, but the mere mention of the word "murder" made me jump to the conclusion that the murdered person was the person whose scream I had heard in the wood last night.

My first impulse was to tell what I knew, but I quickly overcame that. Perhaps the murder—assuming that it was a murder; and there could hardly have been time for an official statement—had not occurred anywhere near Berner's Abbey. But naturally I would think the worst.

And—thinking the worst—I was surprised that I should have had an impulse to tell of what I had heard. Assuming my fears to be justified, I told myself that I must on no account let them be known to Leonora. She had already gone through enough horror. St. Arnaud was dead and no good could be served by saddling him with the suspicion of murder. Leonora's well-being was now my first care, and I must do everything in my power to bring her back to happiness. But what was I thinking about? I had heard the mere mention of a murder, and here I was, jumping off into all manner of wild speculation.

The luggage had been unloaded from the car by the time we reached the front door. I went forward to settle with the driver. Tommy, with that innocent mien which his frugal custom makes him adopt at times, watched me go.

When I had settled the charge, I detained the man for a further moment.

"What's this I hear about a murder?" I asked him. "Do you know anything about it?"

"Why, yes, sir," said the man. "They were talking about it down at the station just now. It was a woman. Young Gregg found her down in the wood there this afternoon. Maybe you don't know young Gregg—the shoemaker's son. When I see him he was as white as a sheet. He had been coming through the wood and had seen the woman sitting propped up agin a tree and had whistled to her—cheeky-like, you know. Then he found she was dead, with her skull broken open. Enough to send a fellow off his head, a thing like that is."

I tried not to let it be seen that I was utterly horror-stricken by this news.

I was actually trembling and I felt that my face had gone white. But the man was sufficiently concerned on his own account and apparently did not take my scared expression as being more than what his story might be expected to arouse.

"And who was the woman?" I managed to ask.

"One of the servants up at The Mount. She's only a girl —can't be much more than twenty. They don't know what she was doing down here on a night like last night—you remember how it thundered?—but there you are! We'll hear more about it, I've no doubt. You usually find that there's something fishy when you get to the bottom of things of that sort. But, by all accounts, she was quite a decent girl."

"Could it have been the lightning, do you think?" I asked.

There was no point in my asking the question, for I knew it was not the lightning, but I asked it for the sake of saying something.

"That's what some of them were saying," the man replied. "But Dr. Bonner says it couldn't have been lightning. And he says it couldn't have been self-inflicted. It's murder, there's no doubt about that."

I let the man depart.

The others, I was glad to notice, had gone indoors. I waited a moment or two longer to try to get back some of my composure, then I, too, went indoors.

I took Tommy aside at the first opportunity.

"I say, Tommy," I begged; "don't mention that murder. It happened in the wood down at the bottom of the hill—just half-way across the valley. It's actually on land belonging to Berner's Abbey. And Leonora's pretty much upset as it is—with the death, you know. We mustn't let her hear about this murder: You've mentioned it already, I know, but we can say that it was an accident and that it happened over beyond the village."

I then gave him the story as I had heard it from the driver of the car.

"Pretty gruesome!" was his comment. "I shouldn't like to be that chap who found the body. Sitting propped up against a tree, you know! The fellow who murdered her must have propped her up afterwards. What a callous blighter, eh?"

He and I were in the hall. Leonora and Jane had gone up to the first floor to see the bedrooms that had been prepared.

"Do you know," said Tommy, "I don't know what you think about it, but I don't like this place? I've lived in many kinds of places in my time, and one place has usually been as good as another to me; but there's some thing about this place that I do not like."

"The occasion is not very cheerful," I said. "There's that for one thing. A dead body lying in a house doesn't make for brightness. Then there's this murder. No, the occasion isn't very cheerful. The atmosphere—"

"Atmosphere!" he exclaimed. "What do you mean by 'atmosphere'? I've never been able to understand you fellows who talk about atmosphere. There isn't such a thing as atmosphere—except in the meteorological sense. When you talk about atmosphere you mean that your nervous system's out of order."

Now, Tommy Gallagher is the kind of man of whom it might be said that he hasn't got a nervous system—like the ploughman who didn't have a constitution.

"Atmosphere, Tommy," I explained, with the air of a professional instructing a tyro, "is a matter of sensitiveness and imagination."

"Well, I haven't got much use for either," he replied. "They're the things that send people silly, aren't they? Sensitiveness and imagination, I mean. It's as well to keep clear of them."

"True enough!" I said. "But I still maintain that it's the atmosphere of this place that you don't like. I don't like it either. But there's this to be said for me—I spent last night in a rather melancholy occupation. I spent the night waiting for a man to die."

"By the way, where is the body?"

He asked the question in the matter-of-fact tone in which he might ask:

"Where is the garage?"

"It's right up at the top of the house. Do you want to see it?"

"Ah! Might as well! I did meet him once, you know."

We were turning towards the staircase. He looked upwards, his eyes following the galleries that mounted higher and higher until they reached the base of the huge glass dome that lighted the vast well at the bottom of which we stood.

"I'll tell you what it is that I don't like about this place," he said. "It's the size of it. It's like living in a museum, isn't it?"

"Just what I thought last night!"

"You expect to come to a room full of mummies in glass cases, don't you? This is a new experience for me. I've lived in many places, but never in a museum. And I do not like it."

"You'll like it less when it gets dark," I told him. "And that reminds me," I said, pausing half-way up the first flight of stairs and turning. "The electric light plant is out of order. Before we do anything else we'd better go round and have a look at it. We've got an hour or so to spare before dinner. You'll probably be able to put it right. I tried to get it going, but I don't know much about that sort of thing. We were scratching about with a couple of paraffin lamps all last night. You can imagine the effect of a paraffin lamp on a staircase like this!"

"Right you are!" he said, and with his hands in his pockets, and whistling a tune under his breath, he accompanied me out by the front door and round towards the outbuildings in a courtyard at the rear of the mansion.

But though he spent the next hour with his coat off, the only results were greasy hands, oily stains on his trousers, and a great deal of cursing.

"No go!" he said at last. "We'll have to put up with your paraffin lamps again to-night. We'll get hold of an electrician to-morrow." So we shut the door of the power-house and went back to get ready for dinner.

By the time dinner was over it was beginning to grow dark. As Tommy and I sauntered out on to the gravel to finish our cigarettes and enjoy the cool air the valley was already in shadow. Tommy was talking. He could seldom exist for long at a stretch without talking. But I was listening with only half an ear. The valley and the wood down in the valley had taken my thoughts back to the girl who had been found there by the shoemaker's son.

I had tried to keep that out of my mind, for my first care must be Leonora I thought, and I must not dwell on things

that would tend to affect my own spirits. But there is something about a murder that must fill even the most callous
with horror. Especially was this the case in the present instance.

The girl who had been murdered was, according to the
account of the man with the car, a perfectly respectable girl.
That man in common with most of the villagers no doubt,
was ready to learn that the girl had been carrying on an intrigue of some sort with some men of the neighbourhood and
had come to a premature end in consequence. He had said, or
suggested, that women who are murdered are usually found
to have been living in some unorthodox fashion. This was
true enough; but this girl was an exception. And it was because of that fact that I felt so much horror when I looked
down at the wood in which she had met her end.

What terror had preceded the end I could not guess; but
remembering her shriek, I knew that, for a moment at least,
she had been aware that she was facing the great unknown.
And she was innocent of any wrong. She had not played with
death. Knowing St. Arnaud as I now did, I was sure that he
had brought the girl there by the same dark means that he
had employed to make Leonora his slave. The girl had had
no say in the matter. It might have been any other girl. His
position had been that of absolute power.

It was fearful to think of that. The man had been a wizard. Every person he met had been a potential victim. By a
thought he could strike the light of day from the life of anyone he cared to select—as he had struck the light of day from
the life of Leonora. No one, except Leonora and me, could
realize how grateful the world ought to be for his death.

The wonder was that more tragedies had not occurred.
That thought helped me to contemplate the death of this poor
girl with less passion. It was tragic, but it was only one tragedy and there might have been many more had he lived. That
girl with the emerald green mackintosh, for instance! I could
see now what had brought her to Berner's Abbey in that
dazed state. She had been under the influence of St. Arnaud's
will, and she had been coming to him because he had com-

manded her to come to him. She had been totally unaware of the danger into which she was walking. Had St. Arnaud been well she would have put herself completely into his hands. I shuddered to think that she might have been walking straight to her death.

I was thankful for one thing, and that was that I had not said too much to Dr. Bonner. Had I told him about my meeting St. Arnaud in the wood, nothing could have stopped a full inquiry into all that I had seen and heard, and the murder would have been brought home to the dead man. That would have caused Leonora further horror, and I was determined to save her from further horror.

I made up my mind to say nothing about it unless it should happen that some innocent man were detained on account of the crime. In that case I should have to speak; but I judged that, as St. Arnaud was dead, no good could come of my speaking.

Tommy and I went indoors. The dusk had now crept up from the valley and it was time to light the lamps.

"Shall we leave this door open?" said Tommy as we crossed the main threshold. "It's devilish close to-night. You would think this museum would be cool; but I suppose that nowhere is cool on a night like this.

"Where are you, Jane?" he called, and his booming voice reverberated up to the topmost gallery.

We found the ladies in the drawing-room. The lamps had been lighted.

"What about Mr. and Mrs. Groom in the kitchen?" I asked. "Have they raked up another lamp?"

"They're making do with candles," said Leonora. "We wanted them to take one of the lamps, but they wouldn't hear of it. Now, come in and try cheer us up. I've been trying to tell Jane how good it is of her and you, Tommy, to come down here on such a miserable errand. And especially as we have no lights to speak of. You must think that we're trying to make it as gruesome as possible."

"That's my fault, I'm afraid," I said. "I ought to have got hold of an electrician to-day. But we'll have it put right to-morrow."

"In any case," said Jane, "we'll all be going to bed early to-night. Leonora's been telling me, John, that you haven't had a wink of sleep since you came down here yesterday evening.

"You don't say!" exclaimed Tommy. "That reminds me of once when I was—"

He was about to start on one of his narratives when there came the sound of a motor engine close at hand.

A moment or two later Mrs. Groom appeared at the open drawing-room door and beckoned me.

"It's the men with the coffin," she said in a whisper.

I returned to the drawing-room and, murmuring an apology, took up one of the lamps. Tommy, well-known among other things for his absence of tact followed me to the door.

"What's the matter, old son?" he asked brightly, and when I had told him he said: "I'll come with you. Maybe they'll want a hand to get the body downstairs." Leonora looked up quickly.

"What's that?" she said.

Then she understood. She rose, clapping her head in her hands, her expression one of fear and revulsion.

"No! No!" she exclaimed. "Not down here—near us! It must wait up there. Take the—the thing upstairs."

One of the men, stepping forward into the doorway, was about to speak. But Leonora stopped him.

"Take it away!" she cried, stamping her foot.

We withdrew. Later I tipped the men for the immense trouble to which they were being put in having to carry the heavy coffin up all those stairs—and down again in a day or two, with a body in it.

But I saw that Leonora must be humoured if she were to get over the effects of her terrible experiences.

CHAPTER IX

THE NIGHT WANDERER

I WAS PROBABLY OVER-TIRED. I do not know. But certain it is that I could not settle to sleep.

The room was large. All the rooms in Berner's Abbey were large beyond normal requirements. But, despite the largeness of the room, the air hung warm and heavy.

After perhaps an hour of turning and twisting, I got up and opened the door a few inches, thinking thereby to create a slight draught. Whether this did actually cool the air or whether auto-suggestion had something to do with it, I can't say, but I did doze off a little after that.

I cannot be said to have been asleep, however. I was conscious of myself, even though my consciousness was existing half in the world of reality and half in the world of dreams. Hovering about in the shadows of my mind were things horribly suggestive—the dark wood down in the valley, with the silent, brooding trees hiding unspeakable mysteries; the sickening greyish light of the laboratory; the girl in the emerald green mackintosh who might have been walking to her doom; the chalk-like face of St. Arnaud as I had last seen it. All these hovered the shadows of my mind—especially the last.

I seemed, too, to be aware of the vastness of Berner's Abbey with its scores of untenanted rooms. That vastness which was originally designed to convey the impression of majesty—to pander to the pride of some former owners—had now taken to itself other qualities, frightful qualities that made an imaginative mortal think with terror of the silent chambers, all with their secrets, lying stealthily in the darkness, shot here and there, perhaps, by ghostly moonbeams.

Then I was suddenly awake. My eyes were open and I was aware of a light that danced swiftly for a moment by the door and then spread itself out across one entire wall of the room.

I jumped out of bed, startled. Then I realized that there was somebody out in the corridor with a light.

Therefore I slipped my dressing-gown on and, hurrying to the door, peeped out. The light now shone from further along the corridor, from the direction of the staircase. I opened my door a little further and stepped half over the threshold.

Near the end of the corridor, where it joins the second gallery, was Leonora. She was walking towards the staircase, whose well loomed like a cavern beyond her, and high above her head she held a lamp that shone brightly on a pink dressing-gown that she wore.

And I noticed that she walked with hesitation, as it were fearfully. And when she turned I caught a clear side-view of her face. It was ashen.

"Leonora!" I cried, starting forward into the corridor.

I was assailed by the most horrible suspicions— suspicions that were as yet too vague for distinction. The least horrible was that she might be walking in her sleep; and though I knew that one must on no account wake a somnambulist because of the shock such an awakening gives, I was too greatly horrified to think of that.

She turned at the sound of my voice. Clearly she was not sleep-walking.

And at the sight of me advancing towards her she shrank back against the balustrade of the gallery. She was trembling.

"Oh, you frightened me!" she said angrily.

"I'm sorry," I said. I realized that my sudden shout and my sudden scurry along the corridor must have startled her when she thought she was alone. "I'm sorry," I repeated, coming close up to her now. "But what are you doing wandering about like this?"

"What are you doing out of bed at this time?" she asked.

Her question was a challenge. Her eyes flashed angrily. It seemed that she had forgotten all the tendernesses that had passed between us only a short time before. Or perhaps it was merely that she had not yet got over the fright I had given her. Her nerves were in a bad condition; a shock such as the present might have the effect of making her turn furiously upon her best friend.

"What are you doing wandering about like this?" I repeated, trying to justify my possibly presumptuous interference, but losing none of the uneasiness that had gripped me when I saw her white face and halting step as she turned the corner.

She found some of her composure, though she was still trembling. She hesitated.

"I'm going to feed the guinea-pigs," she said at length.

"The guinea-pigs!" I exclaimed.

"Yes," she replied. "Let me pass, please!"

Then as I did not move, being thunderstruck both by her antagonistic manner and by her getting out of bed in the middle of the night to feed guinea-pigs, she clenched her free hand and screwed up her face as though irritated beyond endurance by my denseness.

"Oh, will you let me pass?" she exclaimed.

"But what guinea-pigs?" I asked, my vague suspicions becoming more desolating with every second.

"The guinea-pigs in the laboratory," she replied; then as though thinking that some explanation was due to me, she added: "He's got some guinea-pigs up there. I forgot all about them yesterday."

"And you mean that you're going up there, all by yourself, in the middle of the night, to feed them?"

"Yes," she said. "I couldn't bear to think of them— hungry. I had to get up."

"But they'll be asleep," I reminded her. "They'll have forgotten their hunger for the time being. Go back to bed, and I'll come up with you the first thing in the morning."

Again that expression of irritable impatience crossed her face.

"No,'" she said, "I must go up now."

"Then I'll come with you," I stated, and put out my hand to take the lamp.

"No," she said, showing signs of extreme agitation. "You mustn't. You mustn't go up there. You don't know the danger that there is up there—for you. You mustn't!"

"But I've been up there," I said, wondering with growing fear at this sudden alteration in her demeanour.

Out on the verandah she had been the simple, innocent, delightful Leonora of my happiest dreams; and now one would think that she had gone back again to the haunted state in which I had found her on the previous day. I soon reasoned myself into the belief, of course, that my fears on that point were groundless. I knew that St. Arnaud was dead, and Tommy Gallagher had seen him put into his coffin and had seen the lid screwed down. But Leonora's present manner was certainly strange and disturbing. I saw that I should have to take her away from Berner's Abbey the moment the funeral was over. In fact, I thought of suggesting that she and Jane should leave in the morning. The horror that she had been through had very seriously affected her nerves, and this strange behaviour in the middle of the night was one of the results.

"But I say you mustn't come up with me!" she insisted in answer to my last remark. "For my sake, John!" she pleaded in a quieter voice, putting out her free hand as though to place it on my arm, but suddenly drawing it back again, "Go back to bed. I shall be quite all right. You'll promise to go to bed immediately?"

And she had so much the appearance of being in her perfectly normal senses that I promised. Her agitation, I reasoned, had been due to the fright my appearance had given her. She knew what she was about.

I left her. I took a few steps along the corridor towards my room, then turned. She was still standing at the junction of the corridor and the gallery, waiting for me to go into my room. Before disappearing within my dark doorway I turned again and waved. She waved and smiled in reply, and then she was gone.

CHAPTER X

THE RETURN

I WENT TO BED in accordance with my promise to Leonora. When I next knew anything it was broad daylight. Someone was playing a tattoo on my door, and when I looked up I saw the face of Tommy Gallagher squeezed into the opening. The face was animated by a mock frown.

"You're a nice one, indeed!" he said. "We've all had breakfast hours ago!"

"Leonora as well?" I asked rather anxiously.

"Of course Leonora as well!" he exclaimed. "We had it out on the verandah, Quite a jolly party, all things considered. Leonora wasn't as bright as Jane, I must say. In fact, she wasn't as bright as she was last night after dinner; but one mustn't expect too much from a very new widow."

I was glad now to hear that Leonora had returned safely from her nocturnal journey.

"She's a remarkable girl," went on Tommy, coming into the room and seating himself on the bed. "I understand that she was up all the night before last."

"That's right," I said.

"So were you, I know," he continued, "but whereas you're making up leeway now, she's been up since before the lark this morning."

"Oh?" I put in.

"Yes. I'm an early riser, but she beat me by a whole lap as near as one could judge. She had her bath by lamp-light. That shows you how early she was."

I looked at him with a queer sensation in the region of my heart.

"What's this you say about Leonora at dawn with a lamp?" I asked.

That was more important to me than the question of meals. It would appear that she had been up all last night. I could not account for that, and I was afraid.

"Nothing," said Tommy, "except that I met her coming down the stairs with a lighted lamp in her hand. She said she'd been to have a bath."

"What had she on?"

"What had she on!" he echoed, looking at me with an expression of puzzled amusement on his face. "She had on a rather natty dressing-gown affair—pink, it was. But look here! What about it? Shall we waive breakfast? Will you start the day with lunch?"

I did not answer him. I was busy with my own speculations and fears.

"Did you hear me in the night?" I asked.

"Oh, yes!" he exclaimed, forgetting all about the question of my next meal. "I was going to ask you about that. A nice shindy you kicked up! I didn't know that you talked in your sleep."

"Did you hear me shout Leonora's name?"

"Yes, that was it. Then we heard you moving about a little while later. I was going to come in to you, but I didn't."

"At what time was that?"

"Time? It must have been between eleven and twelve. Not very long after we went to bed. Neither Jane nor I had gone to sleep. I suppose you woke yourself up when you shouted?"

"Yes," I said.

I rose, but my mind was not on the business of washing and shaving and dressing. It was on the question of the business that had taken Leonora up to the West Tower just soon after we had all gone to bed for the night and that had kept her there until the dawn.

"You say she is quite cheerful this morning?" I asked Tommy, who had strolled over to one of the windows in the meantime and was standing looking out.

"Who is quite cheerful? What are you talking about?"

"Leonora. She's quite cheerful, you say?"

Tommy looked at me strangely.

We went downstairs together.

I met Jane in the hall and told her that I should, of course, wait until lunch-time before I had anything to eat.

"Is Leonora still out in the hammock?" I asked her impatiently.

"Yes," she said, and her eyes took on an expression of sly amusement. I did not respond to the expression, however. At another time it might have made me happy to learn that my sister, whose approval I regard as a necessary part of any of my undertakings, was pleased to know that true love had survived the unholy marriage of convenience. But now I was eager to speak to Leonora, and so I hurried off round towards the shrubbery.

Leonora was awake. When she saw me coming, she sat up quickly, and even at the distance of about forty yards I could see that her face had a startled expression on it.

I could not help seeing that something was wrong, though what could be wrong I had no idea.

The natural thing for her to do, I thought, would be to come forward to meet me. Or, at least, to smile. Our words on the veranda last night had been the words of two who have suddenly found the world a pleasant place, who are finished with a grim past and who are about to embark upon a glorious future. But Leonora gave no sign of that. Instead of welcoming me, she seemed to fear my approach.

When I was within a few yards of her she got up. Her face was grey, as it had been formerly; there was no hint of the glow that had lighted it up last night. The eyes expressed unutterable anguish.

"Leonora!" I exclaimed. "Whatever is the matter?"

She did not answer. Twice she was about to speak, and twice she failed. Then she deliberately turned her back upon me, and the next thing I knew was that she had burst into a flood of tears, her face buried in her hands.

I went up to her and put my arms about her shoulders. For a moment she was too deeply overcome to notice this, but when she did notice it she shook me off with a wild shudder and stepped away from me, backwards, regarding me with a look that was partly of horror and partly of anguish.

I said nothing for a moment. I hoped that she would lie down again in the hammock so that I might speak to her and try to soothe her into calmness. I was deeply affected by her behaviour, but knowing what she had been through I was able to think hopefully, I guessed that this was the nervous breakdown that was to be expected as a result of the intense mental torture of the past two years.

"Lie down again," I said, "and I'll sit here on the grass. I've got some good news for you. I've been thinking things over—"

"Oh, don't talk like that!" she exclaimed. "The only good news you could bring me—"

She stopped, and stood looking at me with eyes that had suddenly grown steady and a face that had suddenly grown calm.

"John," she said, "do you love me?"

"Why, of course!" I exclaimed.

"Better than anything?"

"Better than anything!" I repeated with conviction.

"Better than life, John?"

"Yes," I said. "I would die for you. That's what you mean, isn't it?"

I noticed that she had begun to tremble. She took one or two unsteady steps towards the hammock, but she did not lie down. She was now standing close to me. She put her hand on my arm and looked straight into my eyes.

"John," she said in a quiet voice that made my blood run cold, "I want you to kill me.

I started back.

"Leonora!" I exclaimed.

She flushed angrily.

"You say you love me better than life. But you don't mean it."

She took her hand from my arm (her fingers had been clutching my coat) and turned her back upon me, gazing away the woods.

"Better than life!" she exclaimed. "Mere words!"

"But, Leonora!" I said, going round in front of her and trying to read the expression in her eyes. "I do love you better than life, and I should certainly die for you if it were necessary. But to kill you—"

I could not help shuddering as I said the words.

"Yet, I ask you to," she said, a troubled expression on her face, her gaze still lost in the distance of the wood.

Then she turned to me with fresh animation.

"I have a revolver," she said breathlessly. "I'll fetch it. And we'll go over there among the trees, above the drive. I couldn't do it myself, but you—"

She took a step towards the house. As for me, I was too greatly horrified to do anything for a moment. She was grimly in earnest. She was so much in earnest, in fact, that she herself did not seem to be struck by the horror of the suggestion. The way in which she said that we should go over there among the trees, above the drive, argued that it was not the deed, but the practical matter of arranging for the commission of the deed that was exercising her thoughts.

"Wait there for me," she called back as she quickened her pace. I ran after her, caught her up before she was half-way to the house, and gripped her tightly by the arm.

"Come back here at once," I said sharply. "Come over to that summer-house, where we can sit down and talk quietly. You must tell me, before you do anything else, just why you have altered so much between last night and this morning. If I think that you are justified in wanting to die—"

I left the sentence as it was. A suggestion that I might possibly fall in with her wishes would, I thought, have the effect of calming her for the time being.

I realized that her nerves were in a worse state than I had thought them to be yesterday. Yesterday's appearance of a quick recovery had been a false sign. She was really very ill—perhaps on the verge of madness. I decided that we must get her away at once. The matter was extremely urgent. I should speak to Jane at lunch-time. We must not allow Leonora to spend another night on this place.

"Now, tell me," I said, when she had, in quite a docile manner, accompanied me to the summer-house and had sat down at my invitation. "Tell me what has suddenly gone wrong, and then I'll tell you of the news I mentioned."

"And you'll promise to kill me?"

"If I think you are justified in making such a request," I said. I spoke the words as though they had an everyday significance. Realizing that she was merely ill, I did not regard her suggestion with the horror that it had first aroused in me. She wanted careful handling, that was all.

I waited for her to begin. I was now quite calm. It was unfortunate, of course, that she had had this set-back; but I could look at it purely from the medical point of view, and I had no fears for her eventual recovery.

There was a table in the summer-house. She had leaned her elbows on this and, with her chin in her hands, was looking away into the distance.

As I watched her, her eyes gradually filled with tears. There was no sign of agitation. Her calmness alarmed me. Had her tears been merely hysterical I should not have worried about them. But as it was, I was forced to think that she was in complete possession of her normal senses and that her trouble was not an imaginary one.

"Oh, John!" she said at last. "I don't know how to tell you. After last night! I was so happy last night. I thought I could never be unhappy again. Surely nobody in the world could appreciate happiness more than I! I was ready to enjoy every moment of the future, for after what I've gone through

I could enjoy even suffering and misery. But it isn't to be—ever!"

"Oh, yes!" I interposed, trying to speak lightly. "When we're married—"

"But we can't be married," she said, her voice coming in the midst of sobs that were getting more violent every moment. "We can't be married. And I must stay on here alone. I must!" She repeated the words with rising emotion and, turning to me a face that was a picture of the most abject terror, she gripped my sleeve with both her hands. "He's come back!" she said.

For a long time—fifteen seconds, perhaps—we stared at one another. Her eyes were wide with terror. Mine, I think, were hardly less so.

"But he can't have come back," I said at length. I spoke the words slowly, and even as I said them, I doubted them. "He can't physically alive. He was dead beyond any question. Do you mean—"

"He said he would never die," she murmured. "And he was right. He said the will could conquer death, and his will has conquered death."

"But do you mean," I persisted, "that he is really alive?"

She looked at me in a dazed manner. It was plain that she was near the end of physical endurance.

"Perhaps not in the way you mean," she said, "but his will is alive, and I must keep on with his devilish work—to eternity."

Her voice died away on the last word, and she sank forward over the table.

CHAPTER XI

POSSESSED

I JUMPED UP. For the moment I was the medical attendant, and that helped me to get over the shock of what I had just heard. But even with my attention directed on the job of bringing Leonora back to consciousness, I could not but retain a full sense of dismay.

If what she had said was true—rather, if she were in a position to make such an assertion—then here was a state of existence of such frightfulness as could not be thought of without horror. For here was a human being—a sane, normally high principled human being—who, throughout the whole of her natural life, would be under the dominion of a man who had passed beyond natural life as we know it.

In the thoughts that went through my mind as I busied myself with restoring her to consciousness there occurred the term "haunted". But I could see that that term was insufficient to describe the awfulness of the case. Her state was infinitely worse than that of one who is haunted, if there are any such. For mark this!—apparitions as we know them (which is more by repute than by experience) have not the power to do more than frighten. They do no more than exist, if they exist at all. They can only appear. They are negative so far as power goes. There are on record one or two instances of persons having been killed by ghosts; but I know of no case satisfactorily authenticated; and I have no reason to alter my already stated conclusion that apparitions are purely negative and are incapable, therefore, of doing harm.

It is in this respect that the term "haunted" falls short of an adequate description of the case.

Her state was bad enough in all conscience while St. Arnaud was alive, for it is reasonable to assume that he had some humanity about him. She had said that he was a devil and she had told me how he had on one occasion kept her awake for a week; but even the worst man has some conception of right and wrong. As an instance of this, I thought of the murder that St. Arnaud had committed down in the valley. He might very easily have sent Leonora to commit that murder. And now that he was dead and could not himself take part in physical activities, he would undoubtedly act wholly through Leonora. I received the picture of a will and an intelligence existing apart from matter, existing in a void. That will—that intelligence—freed from physical restrictions, would have no sense whatever of right and wrong, would be, in literal truth, a devil. And that will, whenever it chose, could subdue the will of Leonora as it had done during St. Arnaud's lifetime and simply make her do its bidding.

And there would be no appeal against its dictates; its power was absolute.

And there would be no way of destroying it; it could not be destroyed through the body, for the body was already dead; and there was no other way by which human power could reach it.

But it could be defeated. There was one way by which it could be defeated. Leonora had suggested that way—she had asked me to kill her.

I was seriously thinking about her suggestion when she opened her eyes. I had gone over the position in my own mind, having assumed that Leonora spoke from unquestionable knowledge. He had come back to her last night, and it was at his call that she had risen and made her way up to that grim laboratory at the top of the West Tower. I could not now doubt the truth of her awful assertion that he had come back. She had not been dreaming, for I had spoken to her and she had given me the impression that she knew what she was about. And she had stayed up there the whole night. The only explanation, other than the explanation that she had given, was that she was insane; and I knew that she was not insane.

For a moment she looked about as though trying to gather her wits together. Then she saw me, and for an instant a smile hovered about her eyes and lips. But almost immediately it was gone and she rose and made her way out of the summer-house.

I followed her, for I wanted to question her further on her experiences, hoping that there might be some feature of the case that would suggest a possible solution. I myself could see no such feature and could only accept the awful fact that for the rest of her natural life Leonora would exist in dark horror. Yet, I could not accept that either. The thought that all our happiness had been thus suddenly swept away was really too staggering a truth to be accepted.

Therefore, I followed her, eager for more data; but I had hardly left the summer-house when she turned and faced me. She had suddenly grown violently angry, as she had done last night when I interrupted her in her fearful journey through the desolate mansion.

"Don't follow me!" she exclaimed, and it was as though I were an utter stranger to her and as though she were filled with resentment against me.

"Don't you dare to follow me."

And without a further word she set off hurriedly towards the house.

Of course, I followed her. I kept her in view until she reached the main door; and by the time I arrived in the hall she was disappearing round the wide sweep where the main staircase joins the first gallery.

In the hall I had the misfortune to meet Jane. I pretended not to see her, but she stepped across and intercepted me, I had not yet considered how I should break the news to the others, and at this moment I could certainly not attempt any explanations. In fact, I should have to review the whole affair very carefully before I mentioned a suggestion of the terrible truth to anyone.

"Hallo!" said Jane. "What are you two playing at?"

"Hide and seek," I replied, forcing myself to smile.

"Ah!" said Jane, letting me pass. "Tell Leonora that lunch is almost ready."

I hurried on up the stairs. I wondered what Jane and Tommy would think if they knew the truth. I doubted whether they could appreciate the truth even if they did not know it; and that thought struck me as being of tremendous significance. For not only Jane and Tommy, but everybody else would fail to appreciate the truth. They would think that Leonora was mad. And if she were to commit any crimes—and she would be almost certain to commit crimes, acting as the physical counterpart of a conscienceless demon—she would be taken and shut away.

Jane's reminder about lunch seemed to me curiously futile.

I could see Leonora two floors ahead of me. She was still hurrying, but her haste was not that of flight; she was not fleeing from me, but was being drawn towards something else. Her face was set into a determined expression, and she looked neither to the right nor to the left, but kept her gaze fixed ahead as though she could, with her physical eyes see the goal to which she was directed.

I kept as close to the walls as I could without impeding my progress. I did not want her to catch a glimpse of me, though I was of the opinion that she was too intent on her own object to notice anything else. She was, of course, under the dominance of the dead St. Arnaud, and her state was probably similar to what it had been when she stood by his bedside throughout the whole of the night before last.

I was a single floor behind her when she reached the topmost gallery, and when she turned into the corridor leading to the laboratory I raced up the remaining stairs.

But she was quicker than I had expected her to be and I arrived in the corridor just in time to see the door of the laboratory, at the farther end, close behind her.

I raced towards it. I don't know what my intentions were. I was wholly impotent, for I had no means whereby I could defeat a power with which I could not even get into touch. But instinct made me want to be near Leonora at least.

The door of the chamber in which St. Arnaud had died stood open and as I passed I had a glimpse of the coffin where the undertaker's men had left it resting on two tables placed together. A moment afterwards I was at the door of the laboratory hammering on it with my fists and crying Leonora's name.

For perhaps half a minute I kept up this clamour, then I heard a noise from within and the door was suddenly opened.

And there in the doorway stood Leonora, but she was a different Leonora from any I had ever seen. During the past two days I had seen her in several moods, most of them uncharacteristic of her; but now her appearance made me start back aghast. She seemed to have altered—physically. In her face there was no single line of kindliness. She was angry, but it was not anger that had transformed her expression. I had seen her angry in the past, and even in the midst of the most violent display of temper there had remained the soft suggestion of that essential kindliness which was one of her chief attributes. But now there had been a fundamental alteration in her expression, and I saw there only hard cruelty.

And, as I say, I stepped backwards away from her, unutterably shocked.

In her hand she held a revolver. It was a heavily built weapon, and as she looked at me out of narrowed eyes her fingers twitched on the butt.

"I told you to keep away from here," she said in a curiously hard voice, glaring meanwhile as though she had nothing but hatred for me. "I'll give you two seconds to get out. If you don't go I'll fire—and kill you stone dead."

What could I do? She had the revolver raised by this time and was holding it at arm's length, pointing it at me so that I could not but believe that she intended to carry out her threat.

I backed away. I had not gone many steps when she came out into the corridor from the shadow of the doorway and, stamping her, foot, she exclaimed:

"Faster! Faster, I say!"

And when I did go faster—not on account of the indignity, but on account of the extreme distress into which the sight of her had thrown me—she made an expression of uncontrollable impatience and fired.

The sound in the narrow corridor was deafening. It was as though a mine had blown up. I was aware mainly of the sound; but I was aware also of the fact that I had fallen, and then of the fact that Leonora—or the person whom I must call Leonora—was rushing towards me.

I scrambled to my feet. My left arm had a strange numbness about it, but there was nothing else the matter with me. And now Leonora was within a few feet of me and had raised the revolver to fire again, this time at point-blank range.

I was not afraid, I had previously admitted being overcome with fear, so now I may be allowed to state a bald fact in my own favour. I was quite indifferent to the menace of the raised barrel that pointed straight at my chest. Other fears greater than the fear of physical danger occupied my mind.

"Leonora!" I pleaded, but I could not say more.

I had had some vague notion of speaking to her and bringing her round from this wildly insane condition, but I could only speak her name. For this was not Leonora. This, in all the respects in which man is raised above the beasts was not Leonora but St. Arnaud.

Yet there must have been something in the way I spoke the name of Leonora for though she had been on the point of firing the second shot—the shot that would have finished me utterly—she did not do so.

The respite, however, was only temporary. There had flashed through my mind a hope that I might have succeeded in establishing some sort of crude sympathy between her and myself; but this hope was quickly dispelled. Her fury suddenly flared up into greater intensity than before, and I could do nothing but turn on my heel and walk away. Had I defied her she would have shot me dead.

So with her exclamations ringing in my ears, I took my way round the gallery and down the stairs. I could do nothing!

It was terrible to be considering her suggestion that I should kill her; but I was seriously considering it. I was ready to kill her rather than that she should exist in that state wherein she was Leonora in body and St. Arnaud in mind.

And I knew that I should have to kill her quickly. Perhaps before the day was out she would have committed some deed that would cause her to be apprehended, and there would follow the needless torture of being shut away. And being shut away would mean that her life would be guarded by the authorities—she would be denied even the relief of suicide and would be forced to live an interminable life of horror. I asked myself whether I should be doing the right thing in killing her, and I called on Heaven to help me decide; and I decided that I should be doing right. The matter was between me and Heaven, and I was prepared to bear my punishment in the hereafter.

Then, without warning the door was pushed open and Leonora stood on the threshold.

I gave an exclamation of amazement and half rose from my seat. But I stifled the exclamation, and my rising was not regarded as being due to excitement. Tommy too had risen—as a matter of courtesy.

And Leonora—pale, but nevertheless the real Leonora—advanced towards her place at the table.

CHAPTER XII

A VISITOR

L EONORA'S APPEARANCE GAVE ME the first ray of real hope that I had since knowing without question that St. Arnaud's power had transcended death.

I had forgotten that there would probably be periods when she would be free from the dominion of his will.

And for the time being she was undoubtedly free. Her own character lived in her face again. She possessed her own personality. And as I looked at her I was amazed to think that less than an hour ago I had seen St. Arnaud in that face—not merely insane cruelty comparable with the insane cruelty of St. Arnaud, but actually that indefinable expression by which one person can be distinguished from another.

"I'm so sorry I'm late," she said with a wan smile.

"I've made apologies," I put in hurriedly. "And we all know that with the worry of the death and all the rest of it you are to be excused if you decided to take a nap at any moment."

As for killing her—now that I saw her sitting at the other side of the table, quiet, dignified, the soft kindness of her face not marred by a single line of passion, the idea of killing he became horrible in its sheer brutality. And yet—when I thought of her as a veritable demon—a demon guided by an intelligence existing in the void, I wondered whether I should not be tempted to destroy her.

But in the meantime I was waiting for a further talk with her alone.

The lunch dragged on. Mrs. Groom, of whom, by the way, I had seen very little, was apparently something of an artist in cookery, and was making the most of this opportunity to show her skill. The lunch was more elaborate than I had expected it to be, and though we had all but finished when Leonora appeared, we had to wait while she partook of such dishes as she wanted.

But at length I found myself alone with her.

In order that we might not be disturbed I did not take her to either the veranda of the summer-house, but simply strolled with her about the uncared-for grounds.

"Where did you go when you ran away from me?" I asked

I was satisfied; from the ingenuous glance of surprise and inquiry she gave me, that she did not know what had happened while she was upstairs.

"He wanted me and I had to go," she went on.

"And what did he want you for?" I asked, thinking it not bizarre that we should be speaking of St. Arnaud as though he were a living man.

She shook her head with a sad, weary expression.

"I don't know," she said.

Then she gripped my sleeve and half turned towards me as we walked.

"You remember what we were talking about before lunch?" she asked.

"About my shooting you?"

She nodded.

"It's too late now," she said. "He knows. He will not allow it. I should have done it myself without asking you, but 1 knew I couldn't. He wouldn't let me. He knows what I'm thinking. He can't help knowing, for he is I—partly. And I would find it physically impossible to take my own life. I know—because I tried it. Last night. When I got to the laboratory I picked up the revolver intending to shoot myself. I was absolutely determined to defy him; but all at once the determination left me. I couldn't do it. I wasn't afraid; it was simply that I couldn't do it. I looked at the revolver. I still wanted to do it. But I just couldn't act."

"But why is it too late?" I asked her. "What is there to prevent me from doing it?"

I spoke as though I were ready to do it immediately; but, of course, before I did that I should have to be wholly satisfied that there was positively no other way of saving her.

She shook her head with the same weary expression.

"I wish I could tell you," she said. "I know, but I can't explain. He wouldn't let you do it. I didn't know that he had control over anybody other than me, but he has. And he intends to get control over you. He hates you. I learnt that today. Don't ask me how I learnt it, because I don't know how I learnt it. I just know it—" Her voice died away to a whisper, and she added, "in the same way as I know so many other things—horrible things."

I could guess how she knew that. But at the moment my thoughts were on the tone in which she had spoken the last words, and I found myself becoming enraged because of the terrible injustice of it all. Surely there was no girl in the world more deserving of the innocent delights of existence! And yet she must be the one to be chosen for a fate compared with which any physical suffering would be negligible.

"He wants to kill you," she continued. "He wants to get hold of you in the same way as he got hold of me. And he'll do it, John! You're no match for him. Nobody is a match for him. You'll find that you are gradually losing something— losing your grip on life. You'll find that you don't want to do certain things that you normally do. You'll begin to find that you haven't the same zest for existence as you once had. And you'll begin to find that concentration and independent thought are difficult; and before long you'll find yourself doing things that you had no intention of doing. It will be too late to draw back then. You won't be able to. And then you'll realize what is the matter. You'll realize that another will has superseded your own and that your wishes count for nothing at all."

I tried to pooh-pooh her fears. In my enormous vanity I thought I should like to try a passage of wills with the wizard of Berner's Abbey, But Leonora ignored my ramblings.

"Go, John!" she said. "Go while there's time! He wants me. He'll never let me free. And you are the only one who knows. He's determined to get you out of the way. He'll destroy you. He's dead, but he'll destroy you. And do you know how he'll do it? Either he'll make me kill you or else he'll make you commit suicide . . . Go, John! Don't wait for the funeral." And then she added, as though to herself: "Funeral! What an absurdity!"

"Leonora," I said, already half frightened by her words, and consequently speaking sharply, "don't talk rubbish! As though I could go and leave you! Let him try his best! There's one thing—you have warned me. I can be on my guard. There might be some virtue in that. And besides," I went on, "the funeral might not be such an absurdity. It is possible that when his body is buried—"

"No, no," she said, not emphatically but with the quiet air of stating a simple truth. "His body has nothing to do with it. His will lives in complete independence of his body. He said that before he died. He told me he would never die, and that's what he meant."

That, of course, was the awful horror of it.

"Anyway," I told her, "I am going to stay here. Whatever you say, I can't leave you. If there's anything that can be done I'll be here to try to do it. You say that I'll have no chance with him—that his will, will over come mine. Let him try."

"John, you don't know what you're saying."

But though she spoke the words in a tone that suggested impatience with my rashness, she nevertheless glanced up at me out of eyes full of understanding and gratitude.

And this was the girl who, an hour or so ago, had tried to shoot me down like a dog! I was electrified by a determination that was surely equal to the determination of St. Arnaud. Will-power was the supreme force behind all this tragedy; I had not thought of the possibility of destroying St. Arnaud's power over Leonora by meeting it on its own plane—the plane of the will. But I thought of that now. And in my violent egotism I had hopes of succeeding. Yes, in my violent egotism I had hopes of succeeding.

We had wandered a good way from the house and were now among the first of the trees with which the place was surrounded.

We turned to make our way back, and as we did so I found that we were in the vicinity of the walled enclosure that had caught my attention on the previous morning. The wrought-iron gates were shut, and the place lay very silent and deserted-looking in the bright afternoon sunshine. But lately it had seen activities, for beyond the gates I could see where a piece of black tarpaulin had been laid significantly over a disturbed part of the ground. Last night, unknown to us, the grave-diggers had been there at work. Perhaps they would be there again to-night. I wondered whether the burial of St. Arnaud's body would, after all, have some effect on the activities of his will.

The funeral was to be on the next day but one. We had decided on that day without having any special reason for doing so. Had I known that St. Arnaud's power would have survived even death, I should have had the funeral just as soon as a coffin could be made and a grave dug. But in my talk with the undertaker I had, of course, been under the be-lief that with St. Arnaud's death the whole horrible business would cease, and had therefore been quite pleased to fall in with the ordinary customs governing the matter of burial.

"Leonora," I said suddenly when we had taken the first few steps back towards the house; "please forgive me! I ought not to have taken up your time like this. You ought to have gone up to your room after lunch. You had no sleep last night, and you had none the night before. You slept yesterday forenoon—over twenty-four hours ago. You might be dead tired."

"No," she said, "I'm not tired yet. And I mustn't waste precious minutes in sleep. You've no idea what it means to me to be able to speak to you like this. But I couldn't sleep, anyway. I tried to this morning out in the hammock. As a rule, I sleep only every other night. I can go three days quite easily without feeling tired."

And presently Leonora rose.

"Here's a visitor," she said. "You'll excuse me, won't you?"

CHAPTER XIII

A RAZOR

WHEN WE ARRIVED IN THE HALL Leonora was there with the visitor.

She introduced us. The girl was a Miss Muller, the daughter of a retired major who lived in the neighbourhood. From the tenor of the short interview that took place in the hall, I got the impression that Miss Muller and Leonora were fairly intimate friends. This impression was strengthened by the very fact of Miss Muller's having called at such a time, for we were led to understand that the call had to do with some business connected with the social affairs of the district, and it would be only a very intimate friend who would call on such business, however urgent it might be, at a house that was ostensibly in mourning.

Be that as it may, there seemed to be a complete understanding between the two girls, and when Leonora asked us if we would excuse them for half an hour or so, Tommy and Jane and I went into the drawing-room to wait until the rain should cease.

I had to put the beautiful Miss Muller out of my mind, however, for no sooner was I alone with Tommy and Jane than they began to question me about the revolver shot.

Although I had hardly thought about the matter since, having been occupied with thoughts of greater importance, I was able to put on something of a confidential air that, I trusted, would assist in misleading them.

"You know that Leonora isn't quite well," I said. "In fact, she's very far from being well. It isn't that she's upset about the death—she isn't a bit upset about that. It is that she's had a—a hell of a life with him—literally a hell of a life. Her nerves are all to blazes. Really, it's the relief at the thought of his death that has reacted upon her. Have you noticed anything strange about her behaviour?"

"No," said Jane. "I thought she was wonderfully cheerful—and self possessed."

"Same here," said Tommy. "I was only saying this afternoon—"

"Well, I've noticed one or two queer things," I said; and it suddenly occurred to me that when the others were present Leonora seemed to be able to exercise a wonderful control over herself. "But then," I went on, "I see her with an eye that is on the look-out for things of that sort. I probably see things that escape you . . . But about lunch-time—I found her in the laboratory doing things with chemicals. She used to help St. Arnaud, you know; and she's got an idea that she ought to carry on a bit with his work. Well, there was a revolver lying there and—"

I had to slow up at this part of the narrative because I hadn't quite made up my mind what to say. Remembering what had actually occurred, I found it difficult to treat the matter lightly; but after a pause I proceeded:

"I told her she must hurry and come down for lunch, and she picked up the revolver—in a joke, you know—and pointed it at me. And the wretched thing went off."

Jane started and gave an exclamation of fear.

"Fortunately, it only just grazed my arm, as you know. I told Leonora it hadn't touched me, so don't mention anything about it to her. I said I shouldn't say anything to you. A thing like that gives one a fright, you know."

We talked on for another half an hour perhaps, and it was only when Mrs. Groom knocked to ask whether we would have tea that we realized that Leonora and Miss Muller had been gone for over an hour.

"Did you see where they went?" I asked, the first hint of misgiving coming to me. "I'll go and tell them about tea."

"Yes," said Tommy, who had been the last to come in from the hall. "They went upstairs."

At that moment even the friendly relations that had been apparent between the two girls were not sufficient to keep a horrible suspicion from my mind, and I was actually contemplating another visit to the laboratory when Leonora came into the room.

"Oh, you've not had tea!" she exclaimed. "You ought not to have waited for me. Has Mrs. Groom been in?"

She was stepping towards a bell by one of the fireplaces, but she stopped on hearing that tea would be in at any moment.

"With everything being upset as it is, you mustn't stand on ceremony," she went on. "I had to see Miss Muller, and she kept me such a long time."

"Where is she now?" asked Jane.

"She's gone," said Leonora. "She wouldn't wait for tea when she saw how late it had got. She asked me to apologise to you all."

It was impossible for me, hearing her speak in this completely natural manner, to maintain the suspicion that had entered my mind. It was perhaps strange that Miss Muller had not looked in to bid us good-bye, but it was not so strange as to cause me uneasiness.

I, for my part, could not maintain anything like the same appearance of careless freedom. But there was one thing that certainly gave me cause for congratulation, and that was the fact that Leonora was not constantly under the influence of St. Arnaud's will. Except for about half an hour at lunch-time she had been free from him all day. When I had learnt positively that his will had remained active after his death I had been visited by the fear that he would take complete possession of Leonora, that, having no body of his own, he would make her his means of contact with the earth and would make her act just as he himself would have acted had he been alive. This, apparently, was not the case; and I had the satisfaction of knowing that I should be able to speak to Leonora at intervals.

My mind was hardly for a moment free from dwelling on Leonora's plight, and up to the moment I had formed two suppositions that gave me some grounds for hope. The first supposition was that the funeral might put an end to the menace that was hanging over us. The second was that time might weaken the power of St. Arnaud's will. I could not conceive time and space in their relation with the hereafter, but it nevertheless seemed possible that St. Arnaud's will would gradually be drawn away into some other sphere of existence and that bit by bit Leonora would find herself being freed from his dominion.

Nothing unusual happened during the rest of that day.

Soon after tea-time the electricians sent word, by way of Mrs. Groom, that the dynamo was now in working order; and Tommy and I went round to the courtyard, where we were shown how to manage the plant.

And when I got to my bedroom I surveyed the layout of the place, for I was determined to save Leonora from spending another night up in that laboratory if it were possible. The most I could do would be to intercept her, should she leave her room, and try to impose my will upon her in the place of St. Arnaud's. I made myself think that I could do it; but whether I could or not, I knew I could not turn into bed and go to sleep knowing that at any time she might be called out to make that lonely journey through the silent house.

Thus I made arrangements for my vigil; and. having put on a dressing-gown and switched off the light, I settled myself in the easy chair, ready to jump up the instant Leonora's door opened.

But the spirit was stronger than the flesh. Had I been able to have a light I should have had little difficulty in keeping awake, but the night was very dark and there was hardly any glow from the windows, which showed only the dull grey of the overcast sky. To sit staring into the darkness of the corridor was just the exercise calculated to send one to sleep. And it must have sent me to sleep—or, at least, sent me to the borderland of sleep.

I came suddenly to consciousness. I had the terrifying feeling that there was somebody behind me—a feeling than which there are few more terrifying—and, though in the instant of waking I thought I must have been dreaming, I cried out loudly and, jumping up, span round.

There was nothing. As I stood for a second finding my wits I was conscious only of the stillness and the silence all about me.

But the feeling of a presence had been so intense that I was almost trembling. I could not bear the darkness. A couple of strides took me to the switch on the wall, and in a moment my eyes were dazzled by the light.

And the first thing I saw was an open razor lying on the carpet by the side of the easy chair. The sight horrified me.

I picked the razor up. It was not one of my razors. I glanced about me fearfully, but there was no further sign of an intruder: Then I tried the door that I had thought might lead through into a dressing-room. The door was now unlocked.

I flung it wide and it swung back against the wall, disclosing a small and quite empty room. I found the switch and put the light on; then I noticed that another door communicated with the corridor. This second door was open.

My feelings were now calmer. I could see what had happened and I was not now so apprehensive as I was thankful that I had awakened in time to prevent my throat from being cut.

For that, without doubt, had been the intention of the intruder. And the intruder had, of course, been Leonora.

I now saw how she got behind me without my having seen her. I was doubtful about whether I had really been to sleep; but assuming that I had been wide awake she would easily have eluded me, for when I went out into the corridor I could see that there were two doors to her room, as there were two to mine.

Where she was now I could not, of course, tell. Perhaps she had gone up to the laboratory; perhaps she was in her room.

I stepped across the corridor and listened at her door, but there was no sound. Yet I waited. I did not know what I could do, but I wanted to have the satisfaction of knowing where she was. I thought about going up to the laboratory in the hope that I might get a better reception than last time. Possibly the laboratory door was open, and in that event I could take her unawares and prevent her from getting hold of the revolver.

Then I might learn something.

But before going all the way up there, I thought, I might as well make sure that she was not in her room.

Taking a liberty such as would be unforgivable in ordinary circumstances, I gently turned the handle and pushed open the door. And when I found that I could make out nothing whatever in the intense darkness, I took the greater liberty of switching on the light.

Leonora lay there in perfect calmness, sound asleep, with her head resting on one arm that was flung across the pillows.

There was no doubt about her being asleep, for otherwise the switching on of the light would have made her start up in fear.

CHAPTER XIV

MISSING

FOR THE SECOND TIME I awoke with the sun high in the heavens. I told myself that the others must be thinking me a lazy scoundrel, and when Tommy came up as he had done on the previous day to give a lively tattoo on my door and to tell me that they had tried to wake me earlier, but had found me sleeping like a log. I thought it time to make some sort of an explanation.

"I've been awake all night," I told him, when he had come in and had seated himself on the edge of the bed. "You remember what I said about Leonora?"

"Nerves all to blazes—yes."

"Well, I'm really concerned about her . . . By the way, how is she this morning?"

"Going great guns! She's certainly better this morning than she was yesterday. Ate a hearty breakfast, and has spent part of the morning with Jane in the kitchen—discussing food, I suppose, with Mrs. Groom. There isn't much wrong with anybody who takes an interest in food. Do you want a complete bulletin—same as you did yesterday?"

"No, no. As long as she seems well—that's all I want to know."

"For if you do I can give you one. As a matter of fact, when I say you weren't down to breakfast I thought you would want to know all about her, so I asked her how she slept and all the rest of it. She said she hadn't slept so well for weeks. Then after breakfast she went to feed the guinea-pigs. Didn't know she kept guinea-pigs. But what's this about you being up all night?"

"I was just going to tell you," I said. "I know what a state her nerves are in, and I have very strong suspicions that she walks in her sleep. She herself doesn't suspect that, so don't say anything to her. Sleep-walkers sometimes come to harm, so while her nerves are bad she'll want watching. That's the reason for my not having been to bed all night. I turned in this morning when I heard Mr. and Mrs. Groom about."

I wondered, incidentally, what he would say if I were to tell him that Leonora's sleep-walking was more fearful than the ordinary kind of sleep-walking—that it wasn't Leonora but the dead St. Arnaud guiding Leonora's body, and that it wasn't sleep-walking but the dangerous stalking abroad of a madman who possessed all a madman's cunning.

Nevertheless, my explanation, I thought, would serve to excuse my vigils and would also account for any strange activities in which Leonora might be discovered.

It was lunch-time before I got downstairs.

I found Leonora certainly much better in appearance than she had been on the previous day; and when I had her alone for half an hour after lunch she told me as she had told the others that she had slept perfectly.

It was apparent that she remembered nothing of her attempt upon my life. But she had previously told me that she suspected there were many things in her "controlled" life that she did not remember, and I had assumed that she was mercifully granted oblivion in the case of the more horrible things that she was forced to do.

She pleaded again with me to go, saying that she knew St. Arnaud intended my destruction. I dismissed that, of course, with as much airy confidence as I could force into my voice; and in turn, I told her that I was certain that St. Arnaud's power would be on the wane after the next day, if it did not actually cease at the hour of the funeral. I told her this with no scientific support, but in order to instill expectation into her mind. Nothing could be done with her until she was convinced that she had reasonable grounds for hoping that she might be relieved from the menace that had hung over her for so long—and that might indeed hang over her throughout the rest of her life.

She was with us for the whole of that day; and, seeing I did not rise until lunch-time, the day seemed to be remarkably short.

"I hear you went up to feed the guinea-pigs this morning," I said, just after we had finished tea.

"Yes," said Leonora, and I thought she gave a movement of uneasiness, as though she would rather not talk about guinea-pigs.

"It must be about time to feed them again," I went on, though I did not know anything about the feeding of guinea-pigs. "If you're going up I'll go with you."

"What do you keep guinea-pigs for?" Jane asked.

"Pets," I said, not wishing to hurt Jane, who would, in common with all decent people, be made most unhappy by being reminded that live animals are sacrificed for the welfare of humanity.

"I'll go with you," I went on, thinking that in her present normal mood Leonora would not object to my presence.

"No," she said quietly. "He would never allow anybody but me to go into the laboratory. I must continue to respect his wishes."

I said no more on the subject, for I was treading on dangerous ground. I saw that if I were to gain admittance to the laboratory I must do so by stealth.

Nothing of note happened during that day, and the night passed without a single incident.

Tommy offered to stay up and keep me company, but I told him that I should be quite all right. To tell the truth I should have been glad of his company, but I would not for the world allow him to see Leonora when the spirit of St. Arnaud was in possession of her. He would conclude immediately that she was insane (she would indeed be acting under the volition of one who was insane—a demon) and there would be the danger of her being shut away if she were to be seen by anybody other than me.

So I declined his offer. But I kept the lights on in my room and in the corridor. And during the day I had taken the precaution of locking both of the dressing-room doors and removing the keys, so that Leonora could use only the bedroom door, which I had no difficulty in keeping under observation.

I kept on the move most of the night, sauntering often out into the corridor, but I was not disturbed.

Once I thought I heard a sound that seemed to come from one of the higher galleries of the vast staircase well that yawned black a few yards off; but this I put down imagination. For my imagination was very active throughout those still hours; I was wondering how I should get on if things were no better after the funeral and if Leonora should refuse to go away from Berner's Abbey. I could not leave her here by herself and I could not expect my sister and Tommy Gallagher to stay on indefinitely.

And if they went and I defied convention and stayed, how could I guard my own life?

I wandered about until the sunrise dimmed the electric lights, then I went to bed. I went with a sense of relief, knowing that before the sun set again the coffin upstairs that seemed to cast an uncanny spell over the house would be removed from the sight of men.

It surprised the others, but it did not surprise me, when Leonora announced that she did not intend to be present at the funeral. I should have been very much shocked had she made up her mind to attend, for I could not forget the fury with which she had execrated the dead body.

About half an hour before the time of the funeral the undertaker's men arrived and brought the coffin downstairs where it was placed upon trestles in the library. It fell to me to conduct them up to the room where the coffin had lain during these past days and nights, and as I followed them downstairs with their awkward burden I could not but be touched by the essential mystery of death and the grand solemnity of burial. I had no reason to mourn. Love, sorrow— these did not enter into my feelings. Nevertheless, my spirit was hushed. The men with their sombre clothes and still more sombre faces, added to the impressiveness of the atmosphere; and even when one of the men stumbled and, recovering himself, exchanged a wink with the man in front who had looked round, my sense of the awfulness of death lost none of its intensity.

Later, one or two people began to arrive. I had not expected that there would be anybody there except ourselves, for the only intimation of the death had been contained in three lines in one of the morning newspapers. And as Paul St. Arnaud had been a recluse for many years, I had not thought that any of the neighbours would do more than remark the fact that he had passed away. But the few who turned up were people who had exchanged hospitality with St. Arnaud when he first came to live at Berner's Abbey.

Among them was Major Muller, a fine old man, the father of the beautiful girl who had twice called at the house since my arrival. I had not an opportunity for more than an exchange of greetings with Major Muller before the cortege was formed; indeed, I had not time for many words with anybody, for I found myself acting as a kind of host and chief mourner. I let it be known, of course, that I was Mrs. St. Arnaud's cousin, and I took care to make Leonora keep to her room, and told those present that she was too unwell to come downstairs. And the last statement was really true, for had she put herself under medical care she would undoubtedly have been put to bed and told that she must stay there for a day or two.

We drove to the private burial ground, which was less than half a mile away. I was in the first coach along with Jane and Tommy, for I was acknowledged that I should represent Leonora—all of which was very strange, seeing that I had been more pleased than anything else when I thought that the death would enable me to make Leonora my wife.

But however hypocritical my behaviour might appear, my feelings were certainly in key with the occasion, for I could not but be struck by the awful impressiveness even of such a comparatively simple piece of ritual as this funeral involved.

Had the funeral been that of anybody but St. Arnaud, I should have been even more deeply affected than I was, for there might have been genuine grief and certainly regret to enhance my feelings; but even as it was I could not be blind to the majesty of death in the abstract. Then I realized that the man they were burying was not really dead, that it was only his body that was dead, and that his will was as active about earthly matters as before—for I could hardly hope that the act of burial of his useless body would affect in the least the power of his will.

And when the coffin had been lowered into the grave in a profound silence, and when the last words had been spoken, I turned to the gentleman who stood next to me—a tall, bearded man whom I did not remember having seen before—and I said:

"Makes one think—deeply."

"I understand," he went on, "that you are the young man who was engaged to Mrs. St. Arnaud before her marriage."

Now I don't mind having grim object lessons pointed out to me, but I do mind being referred to as a young man. Most young men do. I looked at this person to see whether he were one entitled to refer to young men as young men, and I found him studying me with an intense look.

"Yes," I said, and I told him my name. "Mrs. St. Arnaud is my cousin. I'm sorry I haven't the honour of knowing you . . ."

"My name is St. Arnaud," he said quietly.

I started, but managed to hide my surprise in an inclination of the head.

"I am a very distant relative of the deceased," he explained. "I flew over from Paris last night. I return again tonight. Did you know Paul well?"

"Fairly well," I replied.

"He was a magician. Did you know that?"

"I had heard something of the sort," I said lightly. "But, of course, we don't believe in that kind of thing here."

How fervently I wished that I didn't believe in that kind of thing! But I could not do otherwise than believe in it.

"I believe in it," said this tall, frock-coated gentleman. "And if you had seen what I have seen, Mr. Richmond . . . I think I said he was a magician. I ought to have said that he is a magician."

"Is!" I exclaimed, for I felt that I ought to show some surprise at this announcement. "But he's dead!"

My companion shrugged his shoulders. The shrug was eloquent. It said, in effect: "I know he's dead, and I know it all sounds impossible; but it's simply true."

"He has been keeping in touch with me for years," he went on. "Not by any of the ordinary ways of communicating ideas, but by a system of thought-transference. It was with me that he first tried his experiments, and we were soon able to establish a connection between our two minds which could be employed at any time. Distance mattered nothing at all. He has done some uncanny things in his time; and he is still doing them. He started off on the assumption that the will was the supreme power in the universe, and he has justified his assumption. He maintained that the will, if highly organised, could continue to exercise its power after the death of the body. That, too, he has proved to be correct. He told me himself about his own death—soon after he was dead. And last night he told me about you."

"About me?" I asked. "What did he tell you about me?"

"He knows that you mean to marry Mrs. St. Arnaud. He knows also that Mrs. St. Arnaud has told you about the malady that has overtaken her. He therefore intends to kill you. He means to continue his studies here, and he thinks you are in the way. He wants to retain Mrs. St. Arnaud in order that she might do such of the work as requires physical activity, and you want to take Mrs. St. Arnaud away. Therefore he intends to kill you. I should go away if I were you."

Now, all this was what Leonora had already told me, in substance, at least; and though I had never doubted Leonora's ability to judge correctly, believing what she told me to be truth and not mere hysterical assumption, I was nevertheless startled to find her statements supported by another party. There could be no doubt now about their truth; and I was suddenly overcome with hopelessness, for it was now evident that St. Arnaud dead was as powerful as St. Arnaud alive. And this gentleman's words suggested that we must hope for no waning of that power.

But at the same time, his presence gave me a new kind of hope. I turned to him.

"You knew Paul St. Arnaud when he was perhaps less of a monster than he was latterly—less of a monster than he is now," I said. "You are, you say, in touch with him; you can communicate with him. Isn't there some way in which you can influence him? Hasn't he a human attribute of some kind to which you can appeal in order that he might set Leonora free?"

They were waiting for us outside the gates of the burial ground; but I stopped and faced this relative of the dead man, determined by any humiliating supplication to enlist his sympathy. And even at that moment, when my mind was keenly on my appeal for his assistance, I noticed that his features verified his statement that he was a relative of Paul St. Arnaud, and seeing the very marked family likeness, I grasped at the additional hope that was in the words: "Blood is thicker than water."

"Think!" I pleaded. "For the love of Heaven try to think of some way by which an innocent girl can be saved from a life of unspeakable horror! You can imagine what her life must be. You knew him. You know the power he commands. He has deprived her of every innocent joy of existence. You must realize—"

His answer was to shake his head slowly from side to side.

"Can't you try?" I begged. "Can't you try to appeal to him?"

"No," he said. "No. There never was a time when I could appeal to him. There never was a time when he had a single human attribute—even as a boy at school he—But they are waiting for us. He never knew the meaning of the word 'pity'," he said, as we moved forward towards the gates. "I wish I could help, but it is impossible—impossible. I need not say how distressed I am, but—" Again he shrugged his shoulders. "I spoke to you just now," he went on, "only in order to warn you that you must leave here. There is no hope for Mrs. St. Arnaud. Only death will release her. But you— you must go. You will make matters worse if you stay. And you will never defeat him. You will never defeat him. But he—he will destroy you, utterly."

At that moment I cared nothing that the others were waiting, no doubt amazed at my rudeness in lingering behind in conversation with this relative of Paul St. Arnaud.

"Come in and see Mrs. St. Arnaud," I said. "We can talk. Perhaps we can discover some way—"

"No," he replied. "I should only be raising false hopes. I assure you that nothing can be done—nothing."

With that he bade me good-bye and got into his car; and when we reached Berner's Abbey his car did not stop as the others did, but went on down the drive. And with it went my last faintest hope.

I had not thought even to ask him for his address in Paris.

But I had learnt one thing—or had, at least, verified one assumption. Leonora's death would put an end to St. Arnaud's power over her.

And I also learned that Miss Muller was missing!

CHAPTER XV

VOYAGE OF DISCOVERY

THE POSITION IN WHICH I NOW FOUND MYSELF was truly an insufferable position. Yet, no! It had one feature that gave me courage and that gave me an incentive to remain at Berner's Abbey and meet whatever fate there was in store for me. That feature was my love for Leonora.

Without that I might have given up my self-imposed task, for the task seemed hopeless. I had been assured by both Leonora and St. Arnaud's cousin—or whoever he was—that St. Arnaud's power was beyond the influence of a mere human being; and I could myself see no end—except death—to the awful situation of Leonora. But I could not leave her, and I could not kill her. At least, I could not kill her just yet. I must try everything before that.

It was the evening of the day of the funeral. We were now alone in the mansion—Leonora, Jane, Tommy and I. The lights had just been switched on—the lights in the drawing-room, the lights in the hall, and every light up to the very top of the great staircase well.

We were waiting for dinner. The two women were listening to Tommy, who was sitting back to front astride a chair, telling them about something he once saw in Central Africa. I don't know what it was. I wasn't listening. I was wandering about, turning the position over and over in my mind in an endeavour to get hold of some starting point from which I could proceed to act. To be forced to wait and wait in a negative fashion was torture. All manner of horrors might occur and I would be able to do nothing whatever to counteract them. Yet I could find no starting point.

The disappearance of Miss Muller kept recurring to my mind. Leonora had said that the girl went off, ostensibly to return home, after her visit to Berner's Abbey two afternoons ago. But I could not help wondering whether Leonora had been in her right frame of mind at that time. Knowing how complete was St. Arnaud's control over her, I was naturally forced to think it possible that she had not known what she was doing and to think it possible, therefore, that Miss Muller had not left the house then.

I need not attempt to conceal my fears. I may say plainly that I thought it not unlikely that Miss Muller had come to an end similar to that of the girl down in the wood. Knowing what I knew of St. Arnaud, I was forced to consider that as a possibility.

Of course, I thought, Major Muller might be right in his expectations. It seemed likely enough that his daughter had gone off, as previously she had gone off, on a foolish escapade. Nevertheless, her disappearance added to my uneasiness.

And then there came to my mind the thrilling notion of personally getting into touch with the dead man. I ought to have been eager to avoid him—or his spirit, or his will, or whatever it was that gave him the power to interfere in earthly matters. I ought to have been eager to avoid that, for I had already been told that it would crush me, that I was no match for it. But it seemed that only by meeting it—by challenging will with will—could I hope to take the first step towards finding a solution to the mystery.

First, however, I thought that the time had come for suggesting to Leonora that she should leave Berner's Abbey.

"You'll be going back with Jane, I suppose?" I said, supposing nothing of the sort, alas! but giving her an opportunity for stating her intentions.

"Oh, yes!" Jane seconded, with quick animation. "Tommy and I were talking about it last night, and we thought that the sooner you got away from this place the better. I don't suppose you want to live here a day longer than you must."

Leonora looked at us, startled. For an instant a flicker of pleasure shone in her eyes, but it died away immediately.

"I can't go away from here," she said wistfully.

"But you must," said Jane. "You can't stay here all by yourself. What nonsense! You come with us. We'll help you to forget all about—"

"No," Leonora persisted. Then, after a pause, she went on: "There's Paul's work. I must keep on with that."

"But my dear girl!" Jane began.

"Please!" Leonora pleaded. "It's very kind of you, but—"

As for me, I remained silent. I could see that all the argument in the world would not shift Leonora from the position she had taken up. The only way to get her to leave Berner's Abbey without St. Arnaud's consent would be to take her by sheer physical force, and that would be of no use for, if St. Arnaud willed it, she would not know a moment's peace until she fought her way back again.

Jane continued to try to reason with her, and Tommy crashed in with some crude remarks; but it was all unavailing.

"Then we must stay on for a while longer," I said, eyeing my sister to see how she would take this suggestion. And as it did not bring any expressions of delight from her, I added: "At least, until you can get a staff of servants to keep you company."

Thus the matter was allowed to remain.

We spent the evening innocently and uneventfully enough. There was plenty to talk about, and Leonora joined in the conversation in such a way as to make it seem to any casual observer that she was perfectly normal in every respect. She had, in fact, been perfectly normal all day; but then I could not take this as a sign to encourage hope, for at any moment she might be called upon to leave us for some frightful purpose.

I reckoned, however, that her first duty would be to kill me, and I guessed that any attempt to do that would take place in the night while the others were asleep. Poor Leonora! I can say such a thing as that with the appearance of making a simple statement; but it was, of course not Leonora who would try to kill me. Hers might be the hand, but hers was not the intention. The fire that had blazed in her eyes when she tried to shoot me down had not sprung from the soul of Leonora, but from the demoniacal spirit of St. Arnaud.

Before we retired for the night I took Tommy aside.

"Do you feel like going to bed yet?" I asked him. "Or do you think you could stop up for an hour or two longer?"

"If there's anything to stop up for . . ." said Tommy.

"You remember that last night you offered to help me to keep watch?"

"Ah! The sleep-walking stunt! Yes."

"Well, if you don't mind doing it to-night I'll be glad."

"Right-oh!" he said. "Tell me what to do and I'll do it. Are you going to turn in?"

"No," I told him. "I'm going on a voyage of discovery. I might not be long. On the other hand I might be half the night."

He looked at me queerly. We were still in the drawing-room. Leonora had taken Jane further down the room to show her some books in a small revolving bookcase that stood on a side table. I had drawn Tommy into one of the window bays, where he leant against the back of a settee with his feet solidly planted apart in front of him.

At that moment I was sorely tempted to tell him everything. I had no real reason for keeping anything from him except a wish to keep this thing to myself for as long as possible. I told myself that Tommy would not understand, forgetting that I also did not understand. I told myself that he might raise a scare, that he might bring the police, and so on. But, in any case, I did not confide in him.

"Look here!" he said. "There's something queer about this place. I said so the first time I came into it; and I say so again. What voyage of discovery is this you're going on?"

"It has to do with Leonora, of course," I told him. "There's something about Leonora's condition that I don't like the look of. You heard how she refused to leave this mausoleum of a place. Said she wanted to carry on with—"

"With the old boy's work—yes."

"Well, I'm going up just to see if I can find out what that work is. It's all in that room at the end of the corridor—next to the room in which he died. She won't let me go up there in the daytime, so I must go when she's asleep."

"I see," he said. Then he added quietly: "But she let you go up there the day before yesterday—when you had the accident with the revolver . . . By the way, how did that happen again?"

I repeated the story I had already told him, adding, for his hints and questions seemed to demand it, a description of the relative positions of Leonora and me when the accident occurred.

"Well, that's funny," he said, when I had finished; "for to-day I was up there having a look round when I happened to see a bullet sticking in one of the beams on the other side of the staircase—just as though it had been fired straight along that corridor. Funny! It couldn't have been the same bullet, of course."

This made it all the more difficult for me to tell him the truth about Leonora. I could not be sure what he suspected, but I could not take the risk of letting him know that my life was in danger from Leonora. For Jane's sake he would likely raise a scare; but even if I were to succeed in convincing him that no one except me was in danger, I could not be sure that he would not try to settle the whole business by some crude method that would upset everything.

I had formed some sort of a plan, and as the matter was of the utmost delicacy I did not want interference, and I knew what Tommy was. In the case of a physical encounter you could not have a better ally than Tommy; but I knew that he would be of no use whatever in a battle that was to be fought on the psychological plane. And my plan was one whereby I might entice the demon, St. Arnaud, to come to grips with me—will against will. I had to do that alone.

"When there's more time," I said, trying to satisfy him for that night at least, "I'll explain the case more fully. But in the meantime I should like you to keep watch and not let Leonora get upstairs. I'll show you where to parade and so on. Have you ever had to do with sleep-walkers?"

"Yes—once. A chap in South Africa. We used to just turn him about if we found him, and he would go straight back to bed."

"Well," I said, "you won't be able to turn Leonora about. She won't go straight back to bed. It's a rather unusual kind of sleep-walking in her case. You'll think she's wide awake, and when you tackle her she'll show a devil of a temper. She'll probably fight and scratch and—and it's possible that she'll have a knife or something. Anyway, be ready for the worst. You see, she's had a hell of a life with the old boy; and it's nerves—purely nerves."

Then I rattled on for a while about the unconscious mind, and gave Tommy to understand that the trouble from which Leonora was suffering was nothing to be alarmed about, that it was only temporary and would yield readily to rest and freedom from worry.

One of my fears was that they might think her insane.

"All right!" said Tommy. "You're a doctor and you know. I'll do as you tell me. I've to keep her down near the bed-room. And I can use what physical force I like. Good!"

So that was settled, and now I could turn my mind to the contemplation of my own task—though I did not want to give way to contemplation, for it was a task I would readily have shirked.

"Hope we made enough current!" said Tommy to me as we were going upstairs. "We didn't have the dynamo running very long to-day. I don't know whether the cells will hold out."

"Oh, that'll be all right!" I said. "We'll have only one or two of the lights on. One on every landing and one here and there in the corridors."

"Making it more like a mausoleum than ever!" he remarked.

Half an hour later, when both of the women had gone to their rooms and the place was silent, I parted from Tommy on the gallery and took my way upstairs. I had a brace and bit, a pad-saw, and an axe, which I had brought from one of the outhouses round in the courtyard. If the door of the laboratory wanted breaking down I was quite prepared to break it down. And I had in my favour the fact that I need not take very great pains not to make a noise.

As I went up the stairs—further and further away from the cheering presence of Tommy Gallagher—I tried to whistle. I could not. I tried to hum to myself; but the silence oppressed me so that I too had to keep silent. But when, having reached the topmost gallery, I looked over and saw Tommy turn his back on me and pace out of sight along his beat, I shrugged my shoulders with a semblance of carelessness that I certainly did not feel, and set off towards the door of the laboratory.

"After all, it's nothing!" I told myself. "I shan't see St. Arnaud's dead body coming floating towards me."

But in my innermost soul I was not so sure about that.

And in any case I did half expect to find the dead body of the girl the green mackintosh.

With an effort of will I put all these thoughts from me and turned my attention to the laboratory door.

CHAPTER XVI

IN THE LABORATORY

THE DOOR WAS LOCKED, as I expected it would be. Moreover, it was a solid door. I had not observed it closely during my former visits to that part of the mansion, but now I saw that it was made of some kind of hardwood, polished, and that the panels were flush with the frame. It was a door made with a purpose, and that purpose was the keeping out of intruders. It was not a door that could be shattered at a blow. In fact, I was prepared to discover that it was steel-lined.

I set to work with the brace and bit, selecting a section near the lock and at once the eerie silence of the corridor and of the dark still room opening from it all along one side and of the yawning pit of the staircase at the far end was disturbed by the burring sound of the bit as it ate its way into the hardwood. I kept on, feeling a strange self-consciousness because of the noise I was making.

Yet, I told myself that I need not trouble about the noise, which was actually very faint. If it were ten times as loud, I knew it would not reach even the ears of Tommy Gallagher, who was probably listening away down there on the first gallery.

My fear was that the bit might come to a stop against a sheet of steel. If it did I should be forced to abandon the job and seek some way of tricking Leonora into letting me into the room.

But I wanted to get in by myself, for my object was not merely the examination of the room. That, indeed, was not even the main object. I did intend to examine the room and find out all I could about the ghastly works of St. Arnaud; but my main object was to come to grips with St. Arnaud— with the spirit of St. Arnaud—while Leonora was being kept at a distance so that she should not interfere on the physical plane.

My intention was to make myself thoroughly offensive to St. Arnaud so that he might be goaded into some kind of protest, some kind of manifestation, something that would establish communication between him and me.

I could, for instance, play havoc with such experiments as seemed to be in progress. He had kept records, too, of the results of his work. Leonora had told me how she had been forced to measure out chemicals and enter the results in a book. I had thought to get hold of that book and proceed to burn it.

If he had the power of making his presence felt on earth, such a proceeding would be sure to result in a manifestation of some sort. Of what sort I could not guess—I dreaded to guess. But it would do something.

It was a wild reckless scheme. But I was fully determined upon it. It might result in my utter destruction, for I had no means of gauging the power that I was going to try to provoke. But it might result, eventually, in the release of Leonora. Nothing, I reasoned, could be done until I had come face to face with this wizard. What might follow after that I could not tell; but that was the first step. While things remained as they were Leonora would simply stay in her state of bondage.

I do not claim for myself any great degree of courage. It was the thought of Leonora that kept me to my self-appointed task. I had to go on with it. Had I turned back I should never have been able to regain my self-respect. No, it was not courage; it was merely the choice of the lesser evil. I would rather, I knew, face St. Arnaud's ghost than know that I had shirked any duty that might save Leonora.

I know it was not courage, because I remember how often I glanced behind me before I got that first hole bored. It struck me that the boring of that hole might well be the sign for St. Arnaud to act. I had no doubt that in his disembodied state he was aware of what was happening on the earth, for he could not otherwise guide Leonora through involved experiments, nor could he prompt her to try to kill me; and I already had a strong feeling that he knew what I was up to— that he was present, watching me.

My assumption was proved correct almost immediately. From the distant central part of the mansion there came the echo of a scream. I felt impelled to run and see what was the matter. But I resisted the impulse. I knew what was the matter. It was Leonora, called from her sleep to take steps to counteract this danger that was threatening the laboratory.

The scream was succeeded by another. They must have been wildly piercing close at hand, but at this distance their force was lost and nothing but their uncanny significance was retained.

I could picture Leonora's fury at being physically prevented from doing the will of St. Arnaud. I wondered what psychological effect physical restraint would have upon her. There would be on the one hand the irresistible call to her to come up and stop me at my work, and on the other hand there would be the hand of Tommy, against which she would be powerless. Would the insufferable position be too much for her reason? Would she feel as a horse feels when trapped in a burning stable?

I dared not think of her psychological state. More screams had reached me, and I had bored three holes before they ceased altogether. I was glad that I had impressed Tommy with the importance of keeping her down below— glad that I had told him that he might use what methods he liked.

And as I proceeded with my boring, I could not but think that I had hit upon an excellent way of provoking St. Arnaud.

If he did not manifest himself to-night, I should know that his power was confined to Leonora and perhaps that cousin who had attended the funeral—and perhaps Miss Muller. And my plan would have failed. I should know that I was powerless to influence him; and that would mean that I would be powerless to interfere on Leonora's behalf.

And though my nerves were on edge and I had reached the stage where I was listening intently—for what I do not know—and was ready to start at every shadow, I was nevertheless hoping that something might occur. It might kill me; but better that than a lifetime of desolation.

Then I noticed something that made my heart stand still for an instant. I had bored five holes—of about an inch each in diameter—for I reckoned that it would be quicker to bore a number of holes around the lock and smash the weakened section with the axe than it would be to use the saw. And it was when I had withdrawn the bit from the fifth and highest hole that I noticed that the room beyond the door was lighted.

I peered cautiously through the holes I had made, and I listened for any sound of a human presence. I could see shelves with bottles standing on them and I could see the edge of the marble slab that I had glimpsed on a former occasion. But there was neither sight nor sound of any living occupant.

Then it occurred to me that, though I had received the impression that the light had been put on within the past second or two, it might conceivably have been on all the time. I had not looked through any of the holes until this moment, so I was not sure that the room had formerly been in darkness.

Therefore, with this doubtful assurance that I was alone, I proceeded with my work—though more nervously now even than before, and with my senses painfully alive to catch any faintest indication of another presence.

And when I thought I had weakened the section sufficiently, I picked up the axe to complete the work. The noise of the blows was terrific in that silent wing of the mansion, and the wood was stronger than I had expected it to be when weakened by a semi-circle of holes; but at last there was a splintering sound and the door swung free.

There was no one in the room. The sickly bluish-grey light shone coldly upon the stillness. Yet it was a sinister stillness. I was afraid to break it. I had the feeling that I was being watched in the midst of this suspicious silence.

By breaking into this forbidden room I had certainly done enough to draw the spirit of St. Arnaud from the recesses of mystery. I knew that he was aware of my having violated the sanctity of this place of horror. Leonora's attempt to reach me in order to prevent the violation proved that his intelligence was following my movements. My panic was not without cause. I was certain that there was another active understanding in the room, apart from my own.

The locked door I did not immediately trouble about. It was in a corner of the room and was more solid in construction than the others, making me wonder whether it might not be a second means of entrance to this room. I made up my mind to force it open later, but in the meantime I began a more minute inspection of what I saw around me.

The curious grey-blue light—more grey than blue—was, I now observed, more powerful than it had seemed to be at first, and it had the quality of almost wholly neutralizing all the colours on which it shone. I saw a jar containing minium, or red lead, well known for the brilliance of its fiery scarlet, and it appeared merely a pinkish grey. Chemicals that I knew by their names to be yellow or green were plainly grey under this light. Only black retained its true shade. I had once seen something similar to this in a newspaper office, where one of the workmen's lunches had seemed to consist of, among other things, grey tomatoes.

An examination of the chemicals taught me little. They were principally such as might be found in any well-equipped laboratory. I was quite familiar with the uses of the instruments and other apparatus that I saw.

Then I found the book. It was a strongly bound folio journal which had been placed in a desk with a lift-up lid. I merely glanced through some of the pages (it was about two-thirds full of closely written entries) and put it aside while I continued with my inspection of the place. I was going to burn that book as a final means of provoking St. Arnaud to manifest himself.

I examined the marble slab that stood solidly supported in the middle of the floor—the slab across which St. Arnaud had fallen unconscious, as I remembered, just a few hours before his death. There were certainly stains on the edge at one end; but whether they were stains of blood or not I found it impossible to determine because of the curious properties of the light. But I was prepared to guess that the stains were of nothing else but blood.

It was while I was examining these stains that I made my first important discovery—a discovery that very nearly turned me sick, although I thought that I was past being affected by any of the horrors that come within the knowledge of medical students.

Built under the slab was a cupboard, which I had not previously noticed, and on opening this cupboard, which extended almost the whole length of the slab, I found two small glass vessels, one or the other of which was the one St. Arnaud had brought from the wood in the valley on the night of my arrival.

I stood up and examined them, and was convinced in an instant that the worst of my suspicions regarding the inhumanness of St. Arnaud were correct. Horrified, sick, I placed the two vessels on the marble slab.

It is not my intention to disgust others by dwelling on the more horrible physical phenomena connected with St. Arnaud. My business is merely to record. Let me say, therefore, that these vessels each contained a small section of brain—human brain, I could not doubt.

Gradually I recovered from the physical revulsion that had taken possession of me. But spiritually I was shocked. I thought of Major Muller with his words of self-comfort and assurance: "It's all right! We'll hear from her in a day or two." And I was filled with a tremendous hatred against this demon, St. Arnaud.

For a moment my fear left me. It did not matter to me that I was up there, beyond human aid, and that my movements were being watched by an intelligence that might at any instant crush me. I was ready to meet a thousand St. Arnauds. I should have welcomed a manifestation of some sort—physical or spiritual. I felt that no power on earth was greater than my intense anger.

I did not know the girl who had been murdered down in the wood; and though her fate outraged every feeling of decency I possessed, I could not have the same personal emotions in her case as I had in the case of Miss Muller, whom I had met and spoken to. The thought of the charming Miss Muller having been brought here to be murdered in order to further the devilish experiments of this fiend was enough to drive me insane. For I had no doubt now about the fate of Miss Muller. Had St. Arnaud not died, and had he appeared before me in the flesh at that moment, I should have strangled him. I could now sympathize with Leonora, and could understand her fearful act of sacrilege in attacking the corpse that night when he died.

I was about to rush out of the room and along to the staircase to call Tommy Gallagher—for I felt an overwhelming desire to raise a hue and cry—but I paused. For I remembered what was to me the crowning horror of it all; namely, that if Miss Muller had been killed (and I had no doubt about that) she had been killed by the hand of Leonora. Leonora was innocent of the crime, but it had been Leonora's hand that had committed the deed.

I knew I should not be able to disclose the truth, for the truth would put Leonora into the hands of the law. What would happen then I could not tell. At the best they would certify her as insane—though she was not insane. At the worst—well, the crime was so horrible, with its Judas-like appearance of friendship, that I could see no mitigating factor that might make an appeal to the law's mercy.

No, I must not tell. They could never be brought to believe that the man who was virtually the murderer had been dead a whole day before the murder was committed.

Gradually my anger cooled down, and the silent, still atmosphere began to enwrap me once more in its folds of terror. My sense of being unprotected returned. The thought of all the dark, brooding rooms that lay between me and the comfort of human society appalled me. Again I had the feeling that I was being watched.

I continued my inspection of the cupboard under the slab of marble. It contained nothing else except a large glass bowl, which I lifted out—with difficulty, because of the weight—and placed on the slab.

The bowl was almost filled with fluid—water probably—and in the water there was something that lived.

As I looked at this thing I could not help giving an exclamation of disgust. It was shapeless—a dark mass, about six inches across. At one end there was a bulge that seemed to be a rudimental head, and at the other end were two crude limbs. It had no feet, but it had a mouth that it kept always open, and it had two eyes, which also it kept open.

These eyes were pale compared with the body—though the actual colours were neutralized by the grey light—and they were without pupil or iris. I assumed from this that the creature was unable to see. It gave no sign of possessing either faculties or senses; yet it undoubtedly lived, for it moved from time to time, rolling now this way and now that.

A more unholy sight I never witnessed. The creature belonged to no natural species of animal life. There was nothing fitting in its existence. It had not evolved and in its evolution adapted itself to a certain environment. It had none of the natural attributes of even the lowest forms of the living animal. It merely existed. It was no more than a lump of matter that had been given life. And it horrified and disgusted me profoundly.

I had not previously been aware of the harmony that is in all life, of the purpose that lies behind all created things. At least, I had been aware of it only in the academic sense. But now I felt it—felt the beauty that is in the lowest of the divine creations. But I should never have realized the perfection of that harmony and that purpose had I not seen this monster. For this monster did not fit into the divine scheme. It had not evolved. It could not accommodate itself to life.

The truth was that it had been made—made whole, just as I saw it.

And the fragments of brain . . . I hardly dared to follow the thought to its conclusion. That Miss Muller and that other girl should have been sacrificed in order that this loathsome creature might be given the spark of intelligence was an idea too awful to be allowed to enter the mind.

Moved by an uncontrollable wave of disgust, I picked the bowl up above my head and was about to dash it to the floor.

But I did not dash it to the floor. I stopped in the midst of the act. With the bowl held in the air above my head, I found that all volition had gone from me. I could not move. Literally, I could not move.

I seemed to be existing in indefinite space. The notion of time ceased. I was conscious only of my impotence—of my inability to move. Terror possessed me. I wanted to cry out, but I had not the will to make myself cry out.

But I could reason, and I knew what had happened. Leonora and the cousin from Paris had told me of St. Arnaud's power; and now I myself was experiencing St. Arnaud's power. It was directed against me not on the physical plane but by way of my mind. I knew now the horror of Leonora's existence, for I was suffering all the terror that comes to one in nightmares—suffering restraints from which my instinct revolted. I was at the mercy of this superior intelligence.

I strove against it. I strove to make my limbs obey my will. But I had no will. I stood motionless, exerting all my power to loosen my grasp on that bowl, to throw the bowl to the floor; but it seemed that the bowl was riveted to an invisible beam above my head; and though I seemed to be expending superhuman force in trying to drag it down, it would not move.

I had wanted to meet St. Arnaud—to pit will against will—and I had met him on his own plane. And he had conquered me.

In the midst of my terror there came the thought of Leonora. She had told me to go. She had warned me that I should never be able to overcome the power of St. Arnaud. The thought threw my mind into a greater panic than ever.

But I knew that panic would avail me nothing. I must fight against panic. If I were to save Leonora I must first save myself, and by giving way to panic I should only sink deeper within the folds of this powerful, sinister intelligence that was holding me spellbound.

I thought of ennobling things—of the dignity of manhood, of the high moral purposes of life, of the righteousness of my position as compared with the depravity of the will that was opposed to mine. I told myself that I should conquer, that I had right on my side.

But it seemed that I was abandoned by God and man—deserted and left to save myself in a world where space and time had ceased to mean anything and where there were only strangeness and horror.

For, as I strove to assert my own will, I saw how complete was the dominion of my opponent. I was lost again in a wave of terror. Mists seemed to surround me; blotting out all hope. I think I cried out, but I could not be sure, for the actual and the imaginary were now so blended as to be indistinguishable. But a cry in this room would not reach right down to the first gallery, where Tommy was keeping watch; and I knew that my destruction was imminent.

Then, out of the mist there appeared the dead face of St. Arnaud—chalky white as I had last seen it, with the black moustache and the black hair and the dark eyes. Only the eyes were alive. They glittered with demoniac steadfastness, and held mine so that I was unaware of anything else. His body, if he had one, trailed off indefinitely.

And now I became aware of a change in my mind. It seemed that I had given in to him unconditionally. I was no longer terrified. I was calmer, though the horror of nightmare still held me. And I could move. But now my sympathies were with the superior will, whereas they had been strongly opposed to it. I might have smashed the bowl and killed its loathsome inhabitant, but now I was in mortal fear lest any harm should come to it.

I placed it on the marble slab, cautiously, reverently, as though it were the supreme work of the Divine Creator. And, all the time, that face was before me, forceful, sinister, half hidden in the mists, real or unreal, with which I was surrounded. And I understood the mystery of the creature in the bowl. Knowledge was given to me by a means finer than that of words; it was conveyed to me by a process of thought that worked darkly in this atmosphere of horror. A delicate system of telepathy was in being, so that the mind of St. Arnaud and my own mind worked in conjunction.

All this was in keeping with ordinary scientific knowledge—all, that is to say, except one outstanding feature. I was hypnotised, I knew that, and the will that had hypnotised me could direct my thoughts and my actions just as it wished. There was nothing extraordinary in that. The feature that was extraordinary was the fact that St. Arnaud's will had survived death—and the horror lay in the fact that I was under the spell of one who was not of this world.

But the creature in the bowl—St. Arnaud had made that. By a marvellous skill in surgery he had grafted animal tissue to animal tissue, and had kept this artificial entity alive by the sheer force of his own will.

And now he was suggesting that I should do something with the creature—I don't know what. But he was about to make me take a hand in some further operation.

I revolted. For an instant I was granted strength to be myself. His intense concentration wavered, perhaps, for a moment. I do not know. But I took advantage of the instant. All my horror at his revolting work made me spring into action.

With one wild movement I swept the bowl from the bench, and even before it had crashed to the floor I had lunged forward, obeying primitive instinct, and hit out at the face that seemed to hang in the air in front of me. I could do no more than that.

Then everything went black.

CHAPTER XVII

TERROR

WHEN I CAME TO MY SENSES AGAIN I was lying face downwards on the floor of the laboratory. Somebody was touching my shoulder, as though to rouse me; and then I heard the voice of Leonora close to my ear. And following upon the voice of Leonora there was the deeper voice of Tommy Gallagher.

Then I found that Leonora was kneeling on the floor, that they had turned me over on to my back, and that my head was supported on Leonora's lap. And after a while they raised me to my feet and, one on either side, began to lead me from the room.

But at the door I struggled free, and turned.

"No, no!" exclaimed Tommy, taking me by the shoulder. "Never mind about anything in there now. We want to get you downstairs. You've had an accident or something."

"That creature!" I said. "What happened to it? Never mind about me! Destroy it."

"What creature?" Tommy asked, aware now that I was capable of looking after myself.

"The thing that was in the bowl," I said. "I knocked it on to the floor!

"Don't go back!" pleaded Leonora, gripping my arm and turning a fearful face up to mine.

But my mind was not on Leonora. My recent dreadful experience filled my thoughts completely, and nothing was more imperative than that the horrible creature, a work of sheer blasphemy, should be utterly destroyed.

I dragged myself free and went back.

The thing was lying on the floor. It was dead, and an amazingly rapid dissolution was already taking place; for whereas it had formerly appeared to be a solid animal body, it was now turning into a mass of semi-liquid matter—loathsome and repulsive, so that Leonora covered her face with her hands and gave an exclamation of disgust, and Tommy stared, fascinated yet sickened.

No word was spoken. We turned and left the place, and as I lumbered along the corridor, conscious of acute physical nausea, I never wondered how it came about that Leonora and Tommy should have been present then I came to my senses.

"What's the time?" I asked as we were going down the staircase, which, I noticed, was in deep gloom. "And why have you put all the lights out?"

One bulb burned with a yellowish lustre far above us, and down on the first gallery there was another dull glow. Otherwise the place was in darkness.

"It must be about four o'clock," said Tommy. "And as for the lights, we had to put them all out except these two. They were all on when we came up to bed; but I told you the current wouldn't last. About half an hour ago they began to fade, and I rushed up the stairs and put them all out except that one and the one on our gallery. But never mind about that now—"

He nudged me, and I understood that in Leonora's presence I must be tactful.

Jane, on hearing our voices, came out of her room. She was in a dressing-gown, as was Leonora.

"What on earth is all this to-do?" she asked. "Where have you all been? Why, John, your head is cut and you look like a ghost! Whatever is the matter?"

Apparently Tommy had not warned Jane that unusual things might happen that night. But, of course, he could not himself have known that unusual things might happen—at least, not such unusual things as actually had happened.

I told Jane, unsatisfactorily, that I had been exploring and that I had met with an accident. Some day, I hoped, I might be able to tell her more. In any case, I should have to tell Tommy a little more than I had told him, and I should have to tell him at once. I had tasted St. Arnaud's power; I must not let anybody else remain in danger without giving a word of warning about the nature of the danger. Besides that, Tommy, as I remembered, had had to come to grips with Leonora when I started my assault on the laboratory door. It was probable that he now suspected that the trouble lay in something deeper than sleep-walking. Yes, I should have to have a confidential talk with Tommy.

With a flimsy excuse we induced them to go back to bed.

But we didn't go to bed. I dared not go to bed, for I guessed that St. Arnaud—the all-knowing St. Arnaud, existing, disembodied, in space—would take immediate advantage of the slightest lapse from alertness on my part. And Leonora had to be watched.

I decided there and then to confide in Tommy without reserve. The position had become too acute to be concealed. If Tommy should fly to the police, then he must. But it was impossible for me to manage the situation by myself. For one thing, now that I knew St. Arnaud could exercise his power over me I should never be able to go to sleep.

Therefore, I told Tommy everything. We were pacing the corridor, for I had informed him that we must still watch Leonora's door.

At first he was incredulous; and when I began to describe the symptoms that I had observed in Leonora I am sure he thought that Leonora was insane and that I was trying to hide the truth. But when I told him of my own experiences up in the laboratory that night, his incredulity and his suspicion both vanished; and when he met my frank look with a look that was equally frank, I knew that he had made my problem his own.

"But why didn't you tell me about this at first?" he asked.

We had stopped in our walk and had turned and faced one another. There could be no question about his being appalled by what I had told him.

"I thought you might not believe me," I said. "I shouldn't have blamed you for not believing me. Sometimes I almost doubted it myself. I did once or twice suspect that Leonora was insane, with intervals perfect lucidity. But after what happened to-night, I know that she has been speaking the truth all along.

"You were quite right," he replied. "I should hardly have credited it at second-hand. But you couldn't have dreamt all that up in the laboratory. And besides, I saw that creature that you spoke about—saw it dissolving into a horrid mass. Awful, wasn't it? Something—something ungodly about the damned thing! I mean, lizards and things of that sort are—well, you don't want to handle them. But they're nothing to what that thing was. It lacked nature somehow. It was obscene. And you say you saw it alive!"

"I saw that fellow at the funeral," remarked Tommy, breaking in upon my reflections. "I could see at once that he was a relative of the old boy's. But for his beard he was the image of the old boy. Pity he went off! He might have helped us."

"I asked him to stay, but he wouldn't. Said it would only be raising false hopes. He said nothing could be done. And he had to go back to Paris that night."

"Bet I wouldn't have let him go if I had known!" said Tommy. "I'm sure we could have wormed something out of him."

"By the way," I asked, "how did you and Leonora manage to be in the laboratory when I came to?"

"Oh, yes!" he said. "I was going to tell you about that. And by what you say it was a bit of luck that we were there. Lord knows what might have happened to you—up there alone with that demon! Especially when you were knocked out! It was the lights that did it. Not the lights that knocked you out, you know. I don't mean that. I mean, it was the lights that—But I'll tell you all about it. Not long after you went up, her nibs comes out of her bedroom—just as you said she would. Scared me a bit, she did, too! Queer, ugly look about her. And she had a revolver. And she didn't seem to see me. Was going to walk right past. Well, I don't like revolvers. In other people's hands, I mean. So, as she was passing, I grabbed it—quick. Made sure of the revolver first! Then she gave such a devil of a yell! Right in my ear! So I grabbed her next. And she didn't half struggle. You wouldn't think, to look at her . . . I dropped the revolver on the carpet and kicked it out of the way, and then—well, you told me I needn't be too gentle. Doctor's orders, you know!

"I tied my handkerchief round her mouth—for she was screaming like billy-ho and I didn't want her to wake Jane. Then I took her into her room and put her on the bed. She struggled like the dickens for half an hour or so. I thought she was clean insane. She looked it. Her expression, you know. Not like her at all—her expression wasn't. I was worried, I can tell you. You had warned me to be ready for anything; but I wish you had told me a bit more. I should have understood then.

"Anyway, she quieted down and dropped off to sleep. So I left her. I thought I might lock the door, but there wasn't a key. So I just stopped out in the corridor here, wondering how long you were going to be. Had I been able to lock her in I should have gone up to have a look at you. But you said to keep an eye on her.

"Then the lights began to go down. It was mighty uncanny—the way the whole place grew dimmer and dimmer. Devilish uncanny! I knew what it was, of course; we hadn't had the dynamo running long enough.

So I nipped up and switched off as many of the lights as possible, to save the current. And when I was coming down I met her coming tearing up.

"But she dodged me. Those galleries, you know—all sorts of corridors lead off them. She vanished along one before I could get hold of her; and when I saw her next she was up above me. I made after her and caught her up in the corridor just outside the laboratory. But she wasn't such a handful this time. In fact, she didn't struggle at all. She seemed to be quite normal. And then we saw you lying on the floor."

"What a bit of luck!" I exclaimed. "I wonder how long I had been lying there."

"I wonder," said Tommy. "But what's more, I wonder if she knew you were lying there. If she's in touch with old Whatsisname's mind . . ."

"I wonder," I said. "We'll ask her in the morning. She'll probably remember a thing like that."

We continued to pace in silence for another five minutes or so.

"And now what?" said Tommy at length. "I don't see how we can possibly get to the bottom of this. After all, a ghost's a ghost. I never believed in such things, but now . . . And what about that girl—the Muller girl? I'm not so sure that she's been murdered. I think her father's right. She's gone off on an escapade of some sort. Can't think that she's been murdered! That's a bit too thick."

"But what about the two—you know—the two things in—"

"I know," he said. "But that doesn't prove—"

"It proves that two people have been killed," I pointed out. "He had only one of those glass things when I met him down in the valley that night."

He turned to me angrily.

"Good Lord, man!" he exclaimed, "you don't know what you're saying! Are you aware that you're suggesting that Leonora killed the Muller girl and performed a surgical—"

He did not finish the sentence, but wheeled about and stamped off angrily, along the corridor.

Naturally the suggestion outraged his feelings. There had not been time for him to accept the full significance of all I had told him. It had come to me bit by bit—one horrible re-alisation had succeeded another—and my credulity had not been strained. But now I saw the difficulty of convincing an-other.

He came back to where I stood.

"If it weren't for the fact that I had seen Leonora as I saw her to-night," he said, "and if it weren't for the fact that I had seen that thing upstairs, I should say that you were going a bit off your rocker. There's an excuse, I suppose. Things like that are apt to turn one's ideas upside down. But when it comes to suggesting that Leonora could do such a thing as that—murdering that girl Muller and then—"

"Under St. Arnaud's influence," I interposed, for I could see that if I did not put my fears on a reasonable basis I should have Tommy, in his revulsion, upsetting the whole affair and bringing police and doctors who, with their comparatively crude methods, would add innumerable difficulties to my already too difficult task.

He looked at me, long and searchingly; and there must have been something in my expression that made him see that I had voiced the terrible suggestion fully aware of its horrible import.

"John," he said, "it's an appalling thing to contemplate."

He glanced at the closed door of Leonora's bedroom.

"Of course," I hurried to explain, "she doesn't know anything about it. If she knew, she couldn't behave as she does during her normal times. Virtually she's guiltless."

"I see what you mean," said Tommy, softly, biting his lower lip. "He's been using her as his means of contact with the earth—as his means of doing physical things."

"And still is," I added. "And will continue to use her in that way—as long as she lives. I told you that she asked me to kill her. Now you know why."

He said nothing for a moment or two, except to murmur: "What a fate!"

Then he glanced at me with a somewhat more animated expression.

"If there has been this second murder, where is the body? If the murder took place in this house—probably up in that laboratory—then the body can't be far away. She couldn't remove it from the house without our knowing. She would have to do it at night, and you've seen most of what's been going on in the night. Let's—"

"The laboratory—" I interrupted. "There's a door up there that's locked. I bet—"

"We could break it down and have a look. Now, if you like! But I don't think you'll find anything. I can't believe," he added, "that that girl's dead—that she's been murdered. It's too horrible to think about. It means that nobody's safe. But let's go up and have a look at this door you speak about . . . Can we leave Leonora?"

I told him we could. She had no revolver now. And as we were only making a search of the place it would not matter if we were interrupted.

My previous journey up to the laboratory had been made for the delicate business of arousing the spirit of St. Arnaud. I had to be alone then.

But now there was no need for delicacy.

We set off up the stairs. Tommy was convinced that we should not find any trace of the body of Miss Muller. I was equally convinced that we should; and though in this instance I was accompanied and did not experience the same nervous dread at the thought of visiting that distant, eerie part of the mansion, I had a physical horror at the thought of what we might find.

But we had hardly reached the top gallery, from which there ran the long corridor that ended at the laboratory door, when we were startled by loud cries coming from far down the staircase.

With an exclamation of surprise, Tommy turned and made off down wards, three stairs at a time. I followed, wondering what in the world could be the meaning of the tremendous uproar.

Pandemonium, it seemed, had broken loose. No words could be distinguished, and the voices could not be identified; but it was apparent that the noise was occasioned by sheer terror.

I feared that Leonora had attacked Jane, for in that instant I realized that St. Arnaud would go to any lengths to take his revenge on me for having destroyed his work. But when I recovered from my first surprise I could distinguish a man's voice in the midst of the uproar.

When we reached the first gallery we found Jane peeping out of her door. She saw us and rushed forward, her eyes wide with fear, but a grateful expression on her face, nevertheless, at seeing that we were safe.

And then, from the intense shadows at the back of the hall below us, there rushed the old man Groom, his wife clinging to him and expostulating.

"Wait there with Jane," I said to Tommy, and then I hurried downwards to see what was the matter.

When old Groom saw me he ceased his bellowing, and his wife took advantage of his temporary silence to continue her expostulations in a louder voice. But she might have saved her breath, for it was obvious that the man was not taking a bit of notice of her.

Even in the dim hall I could see that he was overcome with terror; and when I had switched on one of the lights near at hand, he held out trembling arms towards me and, in spite of his wife's protests, gripped me by the lapels of the coat.

"What's the matter?" I asked, edging him across towards a settle that stood some distance off against the wall. "What's all the—"

"Nothing's the matter!" exclaimed Mrs. Groom, looking at her husband without trying to conceal her disgust. "He's been imagining things—same as he always is."

"I seen him!" said the old man. "I seen him as plain as I see you—both of yous! I knows him well enough, and I tell you I seen him."

"Who?" I asked; but I need not have asked that. I knew whom he thought he had seen; for I too had seen him, and the apparition had seemed so real that, had I not been aware of St. Arnaud's power, I might have thought that St. Arnaud himself had appeared before me.

"The master," he said. "In the lobby outside our door."

"He's been dreaming, that's what I keep telling him," said Mrs. Groom; but in spite of her air of reducing the whole thing to a very ordinary level, she glanced with a marked expression of inquiry at my suit as though she had only that moment noticed that I was fully dressed.

And when she had surveyed me from top to toe, she looked at me very straight.

"It wasn't you, sir, who was down here by any chance?" she asked.

"I tell you it was the master!" exclaimed old Groom, who was now leaning forward with his hands over his face and his elbows resting on his knees.

He wore an old raincoat, which he had snatched up in his alarm. His good lady had merely a shawl thrown over her nightdress.

I was about to say that undoubtedly he had been dreaming, when we were joined by Tommy who, seeing that no immediate trouble was afoot, had left Jane up at the top of the stairs.

I think that by adding my arguments to those of Mrs. Groom I might have succeeded in convincing the old man that he had merely been suffering from nightmare; but we had to pause and explain the whole thing to Tommy. And then Tommy, to my horror, turned to me and said:

"That's it! Same sort of thing as you saw!"

And before I could convey to him that he must on no account allow it to be known that there was the slightest thing amiss in the place, he had started to question old Groom.

"What was he like? Did you only see his face, and was the rest of him indefinite—trailing away, I mean, to nothing?"

"That was it!" old Groom exclaimed, looking up quickly and fearfully at his interrogator. "You seen it?"

"No," said Tommy. "But Mr. Richmond here did. Up in one of the rooms at the top of the house."

"I didn't!" I exclaimed angrily. "I didn't see anything of the sort. What I saw was—"

But it was of no use my trying to undo Tommy's blunder. Nothing that I could say would alter the sudden stern look of suspicion that had come into the eyes of the woman. It would be easier now to convince the man that he had imagined what he thought he had seen than it would be to allay the woman's growing fears.

"Ah!" she exclaimed. "So he was right!" she said, nodding her head in the direction of her husband, and glaring at me angrily. "And you knew it all the time. You knew that the place was haunted and you never said a word. You let us sleep down here all by ourselves; and we might have been killed at any minute for all you cared. That wouldn't have mattered nothing to you, I suppose. I thought there was something not quite right when I see you going about at four o'clock with all your clothes on."

She continued for some minutes to lash me with her fury. I tried to pacify her, but that was quite impossible. I could only deny that there was anything wrong, and she would not believe that. I sympathize with her; she was undoubtedly right.

I had not the heart to try to argue in any case. What I realized almost to the exclusion of all else, was that the secret—or a suspicious part of it—had been made public. If it had not actually been made public at that moment, it would be made public within a very few hours; for these two would return to the village whenever it got light, and nothing could prevent them from telling that the ghost of St. Arnaud had been seen at Berner's Abbey—not only by the man Groom, himself, but by me as well.

To offer them money for their silence would only be to give the final mark of truth to the story, and I could see that my only hope of keeping inquisitive people out of the way would be to deny everything and make out that these old folks were basing their stories on the superstitions that had been current before St. Arnaud's death.

But, in any case, I could see that it would be impossible to hide the truth for long. Somebody might think of connecting St. Arnaud with the murder down in the valley, and it might be discovered that Miss Muller had called at Berner's Abbey on the afternoon of her disappearance. There would be official inquiries and we would be questioned. And even assuming the absence of official inquiries, we might find the body of Miss Muller.

If we did find the body, could we take it upon ourselves to hide it? I asked myself this grim question, but I was afraid to answer it. Tommy's decision would have to be accepted in such an event. I would dare anything for Leonora's sake; but would Tommy be willing to run counter to the law in such a dreadful matter?

It was now getting light. Old Groom had found his tongue meanwhile and, ignoring his wife's angry entreaties that they should be getting their things together in readiness for leaving, he gave a more or less coherent account of what he had seen.

I was too greatly preoccupied with apprehension on Leonora's account to pay much heed, but I understood that their bedroom door had been open and that the old man, suddenly waking up, had seen St. Arnaud standing, still and silent, in the corridor, looking into the room. The glow from the night sky had been strong enough to show his face with sufficient clearness to allow it to be recognized. Then the apparition had vanished.

But the old man insisted that what he had seen had been St. Arnaud himself, and not his ghost, maintaining, in support of his statement, that ghosts are always in white, for one thing, and for another, that the face was the living expression of the late master.

Truly, the night had brought forth some gruesome developments; and as we dragged ourselves upstairs again I was thinking of Leonora—wondering whether there was now any hope of saving her, wondering whether there ever had been any hope of saving her.

For the second time I went into her room without permission to assure myself that she was safe.

She lay fast asleep, one bare arm thrown across the pillows in the easy attitude that I had previously noticed. She was breathing regularly.

CHAPTER XVIII

A BLUNT QUESTION

IT WAS VERY NECESSARY to keep Jane in ignorance of the truth. Were she to know a tenth part of what we knew, there would be no chance of her staying here an hour longer, and she would insist that Tommy should leave as well. And if he stayed and if I stayed—and we were both determined upon staying—poor Jane would suffer intense agony of mind until she saw us safe again.

Fortunately it is not difficult to hoodwink Jane. The only question she asked was why we chose to perform our experiments in the middle of the night; and to that I replied that the atmosphere of the day-time was useless to us as it was affected by the rays of the sun, and so on.

It is easy for a person with a moderate knowledge of science to mislead a person with none.

I found it not so easy, however, to mislead Dr. Bonner when he paid us a surprise visit during the afternoon.

We did not go back to bed after the scene with the Groom couple. The first dim light of the morning turned quickly to the splendour of day and Jane said that she did not want to go back to bed then and that we might as well enjoy the novelty of an early breakfast. She had to cook it, of course, for the Grooms had gone by the time we got downstairs, and Jane was housekeeper for the time being.

Over breakfast, which the three of us took together, for Leonora was not yet awake, Jane happened to mention the state of the larder, which was lacking in some essential commodities, and Tommy, with extra-ordinary presence of mind, suggested that she should take the car out and spend an hour or two in shopping in the village.

To that she agreed, and by eight o'clock she had gone off by herself for a spin round the countryside, intending to do her shopping on the way back.

We were fortunate to get her off before Leonora woke up, for we could not with absolute safety leave anybody alone with Leonora. And it gave us a clear span of some hours in which to explore further in the vicinity of the laboratory.

Despite the fact that it was now daylight, the laboratory had lost none of its weirdness. The grey-blue lights were out—I remembered that Leonora had switched them out when we left the room the night before—but the glass of the windows had the same grey quality, and though the sun was shining brightly outside, the light in the laboratory was like that which filters through some grating into an underground vault. Here was only the dull glow of twilight, less bright even than the dimmed electric lamps had been—a maddening twilight, suggestive of the ungodly works of a hound of the night.

Of the creature that had perished on the floor only a dark, spreading, putrifying film remained. When I saw this I realized afresh how I had laid myself open to the eternal anger of St. Arnaud, and I was surprised to think that his fury had not already overtaken me. Something I reasoned, must be holding him back. Perhaps he still retained the wit to act with caution. Perhaps he was waiting until I should be alone.

We started on the door without delay. We found the tools out in the corridor where I had left them; and in less than five minutes we were ready to use the axe.

This door was less stout than the outer one, but still we had to give it a number of heavy blows before we heard the splintering sound that told us it was about to give way.

"Just a minute!" said Tommy, when I was about to give a blow that I thought would shatter it. "You won't find a cupboard behind here. At least, I don't think so. Do you notice that it opens inwards? It would have to be a very big cupboard for the door to open inwards. And it can't be very big because whatever is there is built in the thickness of the outer wall."

"Anyway, here goes!" I said, for now that the moment had come I was eager to get it over, I was certain that behind that door, we should find the body of Miss Muller. Indeed, I was so fully convinced that my suspicions were correct that I was somewhat out of patience with Tommy for his repeated statements that I was taking a much too wild view of the case and that the girl Muller was probably enjoying herself at Bournemouth or elsewhere in keeping with her father's expectations.

I brought the axe down and shattered the lock, and the door flew back and crashed against an inner wall of stone.

The cavity into which we looked was empty. It was so small that there was only room for the door to swing back to an angle of forty-five degrees. And then we noticed that it was not a cupboard but was the top of a narrow stone stairway that twisted sharply into almost immediate blackness.

"There you are!" said Tommy. "Just an old staircase. Built in the year dot, and probably not used since the time of the last abbot—if the abbey came up as high as this."

Unfortunately we had not an electric torch with us. I struck a match, and we leant over and peered downwards. But the faint light of the match did almost nothing to defeat the appalling blackness.

"The last abbot must have been in occupation very recently," I remarked.

I pointed to the topmost stairs which showed many marks in dust that had been accumulating for ages. There could be no doubt that the stairway had been used frequently in recent days.

"Let's go down!" said Tommy. And when I stepped gingerly into the recess, he added: "Feel for every step as you go. The iron rail and the steps might leave off suddenly—a popular trick in the Middle Ages. You step down on to air. And you're never heard of again. Go steady!"

I went "steady" for a step or two; then just before Tommy's great bulk darkened the light from above me I called out to him to bring the tools.

"To smash our way out when we get to the bottom!" he said.

"Yes," I agreed; but I had been thinking that we might come to some chamber or shut-off recess in the wall containing that which would prove that my fears regarding the fate of Major Muller's daughter had been justified.

I hoped, of course, that Tommy was right; but to my mind the evidence pointing to her murder was too clear even to be doubted.

We went down and down very cautiously, stopping now and again to light a match and survey the few yards about us that the dull glow illuminated.

So far we had discovered only the bare stone walls, and our sense of smell had conveyed to us only the notion of mustiness and disuse.

It must have taken us the best part of half an hour to reach the bottom of the narrow stairway, and we were certain that nothing had escaped us on the journey.

We now found ourselves in a passage that, we guessed, led along towards the central portion of the mansion, though, with so much turning round and round on the staircase, we had lost completely our sense of direction. There was nothing to do, however, but to follow this passage. After that we did, walking singly, for there was no room for walking otherwise, and striking matches every few yards in order to examine the walls and to examine the ground ahead of us.

The passage ended abruptly, and we found ourselves faced with a heavy door that was fitted with bolts which were drawn back and that was held by a modern spring lock. It was a simple matter to press the catch back and open the door, and when we had done that we found that we were in the innocent sunlight that flooded a room furnished comfortably as a study.

We stepped across this room, opened another door, and walked forth into the hall.

"What did I tell you?" said Tommy.

I shrugged my shoulders.

"Nothing particularly suspicious about that," he continued. "A more or less secret way of getting from the top of the place to the bottom or vice versa. But nothing tremendously secret about it. Handy in an emergency. In the old days life was pretty full of emergencies."

"You see, in the old days—"

Tommy was about to recite some horrors illustrative of the uses of secret and semi-secret passages, but I stopped him.

"How do you account for the footmarks in the dust all the way between the study and the laboratory?" I asked.

"Somebody's been using that way, of course," he answered.

"But doesn't it strike you as odd that anybody should use that way?" I persisted.

"Why odd?"

"It isn't a very pleasant way, is it? Would you rather do the journey via the main staircase half a dozen times than do it via that passage and that stone stairway once?"

"I suppose I would."

It was now about the usual time for rising, so we went to call Leonora and to explain that our domestic staff had deserted us. We could hear her moving about when we knocked at her door. She told us that she would be down in a few minutes, and we returned to the hall.

While we were waiting we wandered into the little study. I began carelessly to look over the books that hid every portion of the walls. Most of them were in foreign languages, as I could see by their titles; and as I am something of a duffer even with French my interest was not at first aroused. But when I came to the section of shelving which held works in English I could not help uttering an exclamation.

"What have you found?" said Tommy, coming forward and looking over my shoulder.

"Something else that probably won't help us much," I said. "But something interesting, nevertheless. All these books are about magic and occultism and so on. Probably all the others are as well. Here's a section on vampires."

"They're birds, aren't they?" asked Tommy. "Bats, or something?"

"No," I said. "At least, the vampires mentioned here aren't birds. They're men—men and women. Dead men and women. Yet not actually dead. Their souls have departed—we'll put it that way. And their bodies have been buried. But they come out of their tombs—supposed to—in the night, and feast on the blood of living people."

I laughed and reached out my hand and took a book from one of the shelves.

"It's a lot of rubbish, of course!" I said. "But there are people in Britain in this twentieth century—a century of free education and penny daily newspapers—who believe in vampires."

"You don't say!" exclaimed Tommy. "I once knew a man who believed in palmistry, and another who believed that there was a better time coming (that was towards the end of the war, of course); but vampires . . ."

"Well, here it is in black and white!" I said, as my eye fell on a passage in the book—a passage that described what the author asserted was an authenticated case of vampirism in Devonshire in the late seventeenth century.

"'These two old women,'" I read . . .

"What two old women?" asked Tommy.

"Two old women," I said, glancing up and down the page, "who lived in a lonely Devonshire cottage . . .'"

"Here's Leonora!" Tommy exclaimed. "Wonder what she wants for breakfast!"

I was about to shut up the book, but I lingered for a moment to finish the paragraph. Then I started on the next paragraph, and turned over the page to see what happened to the old women, one of whom had now died and had been buried with every mark of solemn respect on the part of the near-by country-people. The sequel was the usual one in instances of vampirism. There began to be reports of a stealthy night-visitor to the lonely farmhouses of the neighbourhood, and after every visitation there was found to be some person—usually a young woman—prostrate with terror and physical weakness, and showing a wound in the throat. For weeks the terror reigned, and people in solitary cottages sat up half the night, afraid to go to bed. It was realized that a vampire was abroad; and some, wiser and braver than the rest, formed themselves into a band and watched the churchyard after sunset. They were rewarded, for one night they saw the vampire returning to his grave. And the grave was that in which was supposed to rest the body of the old woman. On the following day they got permission to dig the body up, and when they had done so they discovered that, though some months had passed since the woman was buried, there was no sign of decomposition. In fact, the cheeks were fuller and redder than they had been while the old woman was alive.

The account went on to state how the country-people, in order to end the reign of terror, had burned the body, using so many hundred faggots of wood for the purpose.

I put the book back and hurried through to attend to Leonora.

The multiplicity of the books began to weigh with me—that and the fact of St. Arnaud's having possessed them.

I am not by any means a bigot. I should say, I am not an outstanding bigot. (Everybody is a bigot; self-interest, which is another name for self-preservation, makes that inevitable.) I try to look at a matter from both sides. And before I knew what I was about I found myself looking even at vampirism from both sides.

In normal circumstances I should not have given a second thought to the subject; but at that time there were many things about which I thought twice that a week earlier I should merely have scoffed at.

It is not surprising, therefore, and should not, I think, be counted against me, that on the question of vampirism I was already compromising—telling myself that, after all, there might be something in it.

I was not prepared to think that St. Arnaud's present state was that of the vampire; but there certainly was some kind of abnormal survival about it, and—in short, I was ready to believe almost anything.

Leonora, whom I found in the kitchen cooking her own breakfast with the assistance of Tommy, did not seem greatly surprised at having learned that our domestics had taken flight. The news seemed to worry her, certainly, but I was rather inclined to think that she had been more surprised at their having stayed so long.

She clearly remembered the scene in the laboratory in the middle of the night, and when I questioned her on the matter, after telling her that Tommy knew the whole story and was eager to give all the help he could, she said that she had known I was in danger. She said that St. Arnaud had called her a second time and that, through sharing St. Arnaud's perceptions and intelligence for the time being, she had received an impression of what was then going on in the laboratory.

But the thought connection had suddenly broken, as it sometimes did, and she was left mistress of herself; and having perceived me to be in danger, she had rushed upstairs with the object of trying to save me from harm.

Tommy received this statement with an expression that was a mixture of blankness and credulity. I received it with surprise, but Tommy had a long way to go before he could accustom himself to hearing of things that smacked of black magic.

It was a long time since Tommy and I had breakfasted, so we sat down with Leonora and had coffee and bread and butter.

"Except for killing that ungodly creature," I said, "we're not a step further forward."

I spoke in bitterness. It did seem that the present state of affairs might continue indefinitely—unless the authorities took a hand, when the position would become utterly hopeless.

"But you may be sure, Leonora," interposed Tommy, "that we'll never leave you. He might not find three of us so easy to manage as one."

She cast him a glance of gratitude. To know that she had two other human beings to watch over her must have given her profound satisfaction.

In the next second, however, she was looking at us with eyes that were filled with fear.

"But you mustn't !" she exclaimed. "He'll dominate you in the same way as he has dominated me. You've no conception of his power—of his power and his inhumanness! You will only be sacrificing yourselves. Please! If you go away, you two at least will be safe. It doesn't matter about me. You'll never be able to save me. You'll only come to harm—dreadful, unmentionable harm!"

"Not a bit of it!" I exclaimed lightly.

But in my heart there was not one vestige of hope. Even the slight victory I had gained on the previous night was only an accident, I told myself. The next time we exchanged a clash of wills there would be no accident, I knew. He would see to that. We asked her to tell us as much as she could about herself and St. Arnaud, but she said there was nothing else to tell that was essentially different from what we already knew. St. Arnaud seemed to take possession of her and she was forced to do as he wished. Sometimes she was conscious of what she was doing, sometimes she was not.

"Did you show Miss Muller out when she called here the other day?" I asked, bluntly.

She gave me an uncomprehending stare.

"Miss Muller!" she said. "I haven't seen Miss Muller for months."

CHAPTER XIX

DR. BONNER INTERFERES

WHEN LEONORA SAID: "I haven't seen Miss Muller for months," I knew that the worst had happened.

I was afraid to look at Tommy. Tommy, I knew, was shocked into a complete acceptance of my theory regarding the fate of Miss Muller, for he rose unceremoniously and walked over to the window and stood looking out for a full two minutes.

So the truth was that during all the time of Miss Muller's presence in our company Leonora had been under St. Arnaud's influence! I remembered how she had been aware of the visitor's approach long before we were, how she had risen from her deck-chair and had walked towards the house long before we had heard the crunching of the gravel under Miss Muller's shoes.

And she had been acting under the will of St. Arnaud even after she rejoined us and questioned us about tea. St. Arnaud's intelligence was still capable of considering material questions relating to the safeguarding of his plans. He still possessed earthly cunning, and in this instance he had induced Leonora to act as though the visit of Miss Muller were a normal innocent matter. Only, he had not provided against my blunt question; and so we saw in a flash what had happened.

And what had happened during that hour when Leonora and the girl in the green mackintosh were supposed to be discussing business?

I tried not to show my agitation, though I was horrified by the thought that somewhere in this mansion the body of that beautiful girl was hidden.

I had argued that Leonora had not been given an opportunity for concealing the body. I now saw that all arguments whatsoever were futile. There might be a hundred secret chambers in this immense honeycomb of a place; there might be a hundred shafts dropping sheer into underground dungeons. One might find anything in a place like this.

Leonora did not notice the effect that her words had caused. She sat there finishing breakfast, a naturally wistful look on her face, but no indication that she even suspected herself of being a murderess. I prayed to Heaven that she never would suspect that.

Jane returned soon after breakfast, wonderfully enlivened by her early morning excursion; and when the two women were together, talking about whatever it is that women do talk about to each other, Tommy took me aside.

"The first thing," he said, "is for you and me to have some sleep. We'll both have to stay up again to-night—and every other night until we get hold of something that will put an end to this terrible state of affairs. We can't do anything else . . ."

"You go up first, and sleep till lunch-time. I'll keep my eye on things meanwhile. Then I'll have a nap in the afternoon. We can't both be asleep at the same time. We never know what might happen."

And so, without a reference to the profound significance of Leonora's remarks about Miss Muller, we separated, he to set the dynamo going and I to have a much-needed sleep.

Owing to the dislocation in the domestic arrangements lunch was late. I was glad of that for it had given me a longer rest than I should otherwise have had. I came downstairs physically refreshed, but my thoughts were no more sanguine than they had been. I could see no way out of the difficulty; St. Arnaud's inaccessibility prevented our doing anything. The notion of taunting him and so getting into touch with him was still present in my mind, but it gave me less hope than formerly. Even if we succeeded in defying his attempts to enslave us, we should not be very much better off; we should be doing nothing towards freeing Leonora from his power.

And every day that passed carried the risk of official interference. The Grooms would have a long story to tell in the village, and that would turn suspicion upon us. And, sooner or later, Leonora would be sure to commit some act that would give point to the suspicions of the countryside. And then there would be inquiries and we should find it impossible to give satisfactory accounts of ourselves.

The inquiries started sooner than I had expected.

We had not long finished lunch, and Tommy was on the point of leaving us in order to have a sleep, when a car drew lip at the front door and Dr. Bonner rang the bell.

I answered him, and when he saw me he gave an exclamation of satisfaction.

"Ah!" he said. "You're the young man I want to see. Can you spare me a few minutes?"

I said I would do so with pleasure, though as I led him through into the big library I was uneasily trying to account for this visit.

He put his thick-set figure into one of the easy-chairs and paused for a moment before beginning on the business that had brought him here. It appeared that he hardly knew how to begin.

"It's about St. Arnaud, who died last week," he said.

"Yes," I murmured, feeling extremely self-conscious because his eyes were fixed so steadily on mine.

"He's dead, isn't he?" he asked, and the suddenness and the strangeness of his question made me start.

"Of course he's dead!" I replied.

"Of course he is!" he said. "You saw him dead, didn't you?"

"I did."

"You're prepared to swear that he was dead?"

"Absolutely!"

"Rigor mortis had set in, hadn't it? You noticed that?"

"Yes. I paid very particular attention to his condition—on account of his dying rather suddenly."

"So did I," said Dr. Bonner. "I wasn't surprised at his death. What surprised me was that he should have been able to keep going so long in the state he was in. But I examined the body very thoroughly when I called back the next morning, and I can swear that he was dead. And you know that he was dead."

"Why," I said, "is anybody saying that he isn't dead?"

"Well—"

He paused and studied the floor for a moment or two. I waited uneasily. I guessed what was coming. The spirit of St. Arnaud had manifested itself in front of me. Had I not been aware of the extraordinary possibilities that lay behind St. Arnaud's unique will, I should have thought that I had seen him in the flesh. He had shown himself to the old man Groom. He might have shown himself to others.

"Your servants have gone," Dr. Bonner remarked, looking up at me. "They both say they saw St. Arnaud walking about the place in the night. Last night."

"Both of them?"

"Yes. And they say that you saw him. Did you?"

"I thought I did. Probably imagination."

"I would like you to tell me all about it. For the woman in the post office said she saw him as she was walking home last night. You can't all be imagining the same thing."

Here it was—the beginning of the inquiry! How could I ever have thought to keep the affair secret! They would find out that though St. Arnaud's body was dead his will was still active—as he had prophesied it would be. And then they would find out that he had Leonora under his control and could force her to commit any crime. And so they would take Leonora away.

"Doctor," I said, " let me tell you everything. I wish I had told you at first, but I thought that his death would put an end to all the horror. It's too late now. But perhaps it isn't. If there's any truth in the records of vampirism, it might not yet be too late. You might know—Just a minute! Let me fetch my brother-in-law. He has seen some of the queer things that have been going on."

Fortunately Tommy had not gone to bed. I found him in his room and brought him down to the library.

"What's that you were saying about vampirism?" asked Dr. Bonner when I had introduced the two men. "You don't mean that you believe in fairy tales of that sort!"

"I believe in lots of things that I never thought I should believe in," I told him. "When you've heard everything, Doctor, I'll take you through to the study and show you a few of St. Arnaud's books on magic."

"Magic!"

The doctor looked at me queerly, and I thought I had better not test his credulity too much until I had recounted all that had happened since my coming down from London.

For I had made up my mind to tell him everything. To try to conceal any of the essential facts would merely land me in a hopeless muddle. If I told him everything he might be able to discover a way out. He was, I thought, a humane man. He would realize the horror of our position and would try to help. And, in any case, we could not for long keep the horrible secret to ourselves.

He let me proceed without interruption, although the recital of the essential facts of the case took me well over an hour.

And when I had concluded, after bringing the case up to that very morning, when Leonora had made her unconsciously significant statement over the breakfast-table, he still sat where he was, deep in thought, it seemed, and making no comment on all I had told him.

At length he rose.

"What do you think about it?" I asked.

His only reply was to shrug his shoulders. Then as he took a step towards the door, he said:

"You mentioned some books—some books on vampirism."

"Oh, yes!" I said, and led the way out of the library and round towards the study.

I could not tell what he was thinking. I believed, judging by his manner, that he had accepted my story as the absolute truth; but whether he had formed any theory of his own or whether he had any hope of destroying the spirit of St. Arnaud I could not guess.

We stayed in the study for another half an hour or longer. During that time the doctor took down numerous books and glanced through them, sometimes putting them back immediately, sometimes reading whole pages.

"Take me up to the laboratory, will you?" he said at length.

But when we were out in the hall again, he paused.

"If Mrs. St. Arnaud is disengaged," he said, " I should like to have a look at her. Is she somewhere about?"

In the drawing-room we found Jane.

"Leonora went off upstairs nearly an hour ago," said Jane in answer to our inquiries. "Rushed off in the most curious way," she added, rising and coming out into the hall.

We three men exchanged glances. We could not help it.

It was necessary to expend some moments in introducing the doctor to Jane, but we hurried off as quickly as we could without exciting Jane's suspicions.

We were too late, however, to discover Leonora actually engaged on St. Arnaud's work. We met her coming down when we were about half way up.

She seemed slightly agitated, but there was no suggestion of violence about her. She did not show surprise at seeing Dr. Bonner, though she had not been aware, so far as I knew, of his arrival. Nor did she appear be curious about the business that was taking us upstairs.

The doctor spoke to her about general things—the merest small-talk. Never once did he mention the terrible horror that was hanging over us all, but I noticed that he was observing Leonora closely all the time he was talking to her.

At the first opportunity, she turned to me.

"Did you take a book out of the laboratory?" she asked, and by the eagerness of her question she showed that the book was the principal matter in her mind at that moment.

"A big journal?" I asked. "No; it was there this morning."

I had intended to destroy that book.

"Not that one," she said. "One like it. That one is up there now. It's the other one that's lost. It's the important one—the one that's lost." Her agitation had increased while she was speaking. It was easy to see that she was acting under some volition not quite her own. I glanced at Dr. Bonner. He was studying her more keenly than ever.

She made to continue on her way downstairs. Tommy, with a meaning look at me, turned and accompanied her.

The doctor and I went on up towards the laboratory.

"There's something uncanny going on in this house," he said, but though I asked him again what he thought about it, he would not risk a more definite remark. In the laboratory I showed him all that could possibly be of interest. He confirmed my observations on the contents of the two glass containers that still stood on the marble slab. As he looked at them his eyes lit up with a sudden blaze of anger, then he turned from them with an expression of disgust on his face.

"We must preserve these," he said. "The police will want to see them."

"Are you going to bring the police here?" I asked, a wave of terror coming over me. "But she's innocent. She may have committed one of the murders, but she's innocent, nevertheless."

"That may be," he said. "But you can't keep the police out of it—not when you've things like that lying about the place."

He jerked his head in the direction of the marble slab and, going over to the desk, opened the book and started to examine a page here and there.

I stood looking on, helpless. I had given Dr. Bonner my confidence and he, with a mind working along orthodox lines, was going to give the facts to the police. The police would ignore everything in the story that they could not understand—and the proof of Leonora's innocence lay in realms of knowledge that doctors, to say nothing of policemen, did not understand. I could see nothing but disaster ahead. I wished that I had killed Leonora when she asked me to; and, of course, killed myself as well. I might still do that, I told myself, if St. Arnaud did not arrest my hand as he had arrested it when I first tried to smash that glass bowl.

"You'll be waiting up to-night, I suppose?" asked Dr. Bonner, shutting the book and turning towards me.

I said that we should.

"Then, if you don't mind," he said, sauntering towards the door, "I'll come back in the evening and keep you company."

"Oh, do!" I said, glad of any word of hope from a higher authority.

"Do you think you have discovered anything? I mean, have you any theory?"

He would not venture an opinion. I was disappointed, but I did not think him unreasonable not to share his thoughts with me. The whole matter was one that discouraged the making of definite assertions.

"I should like to observe Mrs. St. Arnaud a little more closely," he said.

Ten minutes later he took his leave.

CHAPTER XX

THE BURIAL GROUND

I SPENT THE REST OF THAT DAY in a frame of mind that was a mixture of hope and despair. I was moved by an acute feeling of expectation. I usually look askance on feelings that have not a reasonable basis. I set no stone by premonitions. But to-day I was unaccountably convinced that something was going to happen.

Most of the afternoon I spent in the company of Leonora and Jane, neither of whom showed any particular curiosity respecting the visit of Dr. Bonner. I did not have an opportunity for any private conversation with Leonora; and for that I was glad, because I did not want to say anything that might lead her to think that she was under the doctor's observation.

When Tommy came down I slipped away into the study, where I spent some hours in perusing books on vampirism and subjects dealing with after-death manifestations.

The more I thought about the matter the more probable it seemed to me that somewhere in this collection of books there would be hidden the key that would solve the present mystery. Unless St. Arnaud's case were unique among the supernatural happenings within the knowledge of mankind, there must, I reasoned, be a reference to a similar case—and there might be shown a method of dealing with it.

But the records of supernatural manifestations seemed endless in their number and their variety; and when I was called to dinner I had discovered only one remedy that seemed to be commonly relied upon in cases of earthly survival after death, and that remedy was the same as had been mentioned in the instance of the woman vampire—namely, the burning of the material body.

When Dr. Bonner did arrive, we were ready for him; and without a hitch the three of us found ourselves stationed about my bedroom door, prepared for anything that might happen.

Our only fear was that nothing would happen.

We arranged that should Leonora come out of her room Dr. Bonner and I should follow her, and that Tommy should stay behind to look after Jane.

St. Arnaud had been very quiet all day, in a manner of speaking. But there was no doubt of his being aware of the destruction of the creature he had made, and there was no doubt that he would try to take his revenge. It was quite conceivable that his revenge might include some harm to Jane, therefore we dared not leave her unprotected.

"Has she been up to feed the guinea-pigs to-day?" Tommy whispered.

"There aren't any guinea pigs," I told him. "That was only an excuse for being allowed to make that first journey in the night . . . Ssh—!"

Leonora's door opened slowly and she stepped cautiously out into the corridor.

We were standing in the half-dark doorway of my room, but we could not have been overlooked by any normally waking person who might pass along the corridor. Dr. Bonner, who was nearest the threshold, started back, but I whispered to him that she would not notice us. And she didn't.

Her expression was set. It was more like the expression of an ordinary sleep-walker than was usual in her case. There was no suggestion of the insane cruelty of St. Arnaud in her face. She was quite unconscious of us, even though, as she turned, her eyes swept our doorway.

From these signs I guessed that she was deeply under St. Arnaud's influence and that she was not bound on any work of revenge. Had her intention been to kill me, that terrible unnatural look of hatred would have been on her face.

Another noticeable feature was that she was fully dressed. That is to say, she had on the light frock that she had worn during the afternoon. Hitherto, she had worn a dressing-gown on her night journeys.

We let her get to the end of the corridor, then we slipped out after her, leaving Tommy to go to his own room.

Instead of making for the laboratory as she usually did, Leonora turned downwards in the direction of the hall.

The doctor made a sound of annoyance.

"Nothing more than sleep-walking!" he murmured. "Clearly a case of sleep-walking!"

"We'll see," I whispered.

We followed her down the staircase. When she reached the bottom she walked, with her head held high, straight across the hall to the front door.

I was surprised at this departure from her usual custom, for hitherto her unconscious duties seemed to have taken her to the laboratory.

I could not, however, form any guess at her intentions, and could merely watch her.

Noiselessly she undid the only bolt that was fastened, and, turning the key, opened the door a few inches and slipped out into the night.

We hurried after her.

For my part I was intensely excited and was fearful lest we might lose sight of her in the blackness of the night—for the sky was completely overcast. The doctor, however, did not seem to share my excitement. As we stood for a moment on the topmost step, watching the faint whiteness of her dress as she walked slowly along by the front of the house, the doctor grunted a number of times and murmured something about sleep-walking.

We went down after her, instinctively treading with wariness though we knew that a noise would not divert her from her object.

She continued right along the front of the house, bearing herself with a queenly dignity that made the indefinable whiteness of her dress seem ghostly in the midst of the black shadows. At the end of the house she turned through the wide archway that led to the courtyard wherein were situated all the outbuildings.

We hurried so as not to lose sight of her, and were in time to see her disappear within one of the open doorways. We were half way across the courtyard, intending to follow her into the building, when her white form reappeared. Quickly we slipped back into the deep shadows by the main archway, and she passed within a few feet of us, returning by the way she had come.

"What was she carrying?" Dr. Bonner whispered as we crept out stealthily from the shadows.

"You saw what she was carrying!" I said, my voice unnecessarily harsh, as though I were accusing him of being afraid to admit what he had seen.

"A spade, was it?"

"Yes," I said. "A spade."

A thousand horrible apprehensions ran through my mind as we followed her out into the open. The chief of these had to do with the body of Miss Muller. The body was concealed somewhere, temporarily, I guessed, and she was now going to bury it. And some such thoughts were occupying the doctor's mind, I suspected, for he had ceased to grunt and to murmur about sleep-walking.

The white form of Leonora had now turned away from the house, and as I realized the direction it was taking, I could not help gripping the doctor's arm.

"Doctor!" I said, fearfully. "Do you see where she's going?"

"No," he replied. "Where?"

"To the burial ground!"

I cannot attempt to describe the horror with which this truth struck me. For there could be no doubt about the direction in which Leonora was going. Although the night was pitch black I was sufficiently well aware of my bearings to know that she was making for the road along which the funeral cortege had passed a day or two earlier.

I had ceased to speculate consciously on her intentions. I could but follow, knowing nothing but profound fear and horror. The significance of the spade in conjunction with the burial ground that I could imagine lying still and silent under the black night sky conjured up visions of inexpressible mystery. At moments I was constrained to rush forward and stop her; but reason told me that we must let her go on in order that we might find out anything that might help us to lay the ghost of the wizard of Berner's Abbey.

I did not see how our spying on Leonora while she dug a grave for the body of her victim could help us to counter the menace, but I followed—trembling, horrified to think that a girl like Leonora should be engaged, even unconsciously, in such ghastly work.

She came at length to the comparatively clear space surrounding the burial ground; but even where there were no overhanging trees it was difficult to distinguish anything.

We saw the white of her form approach the wrought-iron gates, and a moment later she had disappeared within. We followed, noiselessly; and when we looked around inside, we caught a glimpse of her threading her way amongst the tombs.

She stopped by the newly filled grave of St. Arnaud.

Dr. Bonner clutched my arm and dragged me quickly behind an elaborate tombstone that stood perhaps fifteen yards from where Leonora had paused.

"Look!" he whispered. "Somebody else is there!"

I stared into the darkness, and though I could hardly believe my eyes, I certainly became aware of another figure—a dim, black figure—that seemed to have materialized out of the ground.

All that I had read about vampires became for me unquestionably true. I had no doubt that the dim figure—the figure that appeared just a shade blacker than the surrounding blackness—was that of St. Arnaud.

I made a movement as though to free myself from the grip of the doctor, but he held me tightly.

"Don't make a noise!" he breathed. "Just watch!"

"But he might—!"

"I don't think she'll come to any harm," he assured me. "In any case, we can be with her in a couple of seconds."

"Who is it?" I asked, wondering whether he had reached the same conclusion as I. During the afternoon he had certainly seemed deeply interested in the books on vampirism.

He did not reply.

In the meantime there had come to our ears the unmistakable sound of a spade at work. Someone was opening the grave.

"I'll crawl forward," I said, unable to remain still any longer. "I'll try to get a better view of what's going on."

He hesitated a moment before replying.

"Very well!" he said, at length. "But for Heaven's sake don't let yourself be seen! And don't do anything. If you disturb them we'll be no further forward than before."

I promised and, crouching low on hands and knees, I wormed myself towards the tombstone nearest to where the operations were being carried on.

Though I was now within five yards of them and dared not go any nearer, I found it difficult to pierce the blackness. All that I could be sure of was the dim whiteness of Leonora's dress and the vagueness of that other presence. Whether that other were matter or spirit I could not tell.

But I had faith in my suspicions. I knew, without proof, that the other was St. Arnaud, and a wave of terror swept over me with the realization that the dead could rise, could manifest themselves, could disturb their own graves.

I crept back to the doctor, loath to leave Leonora alone among the dead—the active dead—but remembering the doctor's injunction not to interfere with what was afoot.

"It's St. Arnaud," I said, not thinking that I was taking anything for granted.

"I thought so," he remarked, and from that I knew that his thoughts had followed the same line as mine—that he too had come to a belief in the vampire legend.

We waited motionless for hours.

The thought of a grave being opened was at first a revolting thought, but I soon became intent on the question of why the grave should be opened. The vampire stories came to my mind. It was possible that to be tied to the earth was torture for a disembodied spirit. It was possible that St. Arnaud had realized this and was now taking the only effective measure he knew in order to free himself from his bondage. He was causing Leonora to disinter his dead body, drag it up to the laboratory and there destroy it by fire. That seemed quite feasible to me as I crouched there behind the tombstone.

Then, after hours of waiting, there came the sound of the spade striking wood.

The doctor gripped my arm.

"Let's both creep forward," he whispered. "You go first. You know the way. Not a sound!"

He was tremendously excited.

Without a word I crept forward and, threading my way as before, took up my position behind the tombstone nearest to the opened grave. The doctor was at my back.

The sound of the digging had now ceased. Other sounds came to us—indefinable sounds of exertion. The coffin was being opened.

Then a ghastly radiance lit up the scene. To our eyes, accustomed now to intense darkness, it seemed that the grave was filled with light. And this light, shooting upwards, illuminated the face and shoulders of Leonora, whom we saw to be kneeling on the ground, looking over into the grisly pit.

"Now!" exclaimed Dr. Bonner, and jumping to his feet, he rushed forward.

I followed, reckless of noise. Yet, in that wild moment, I noticed that Leonora never moved. She seemed not to notice us.

The light suddenly went out. But another—from a torch in the doctor's hand—illuminated the whole scene.

And out of the grave at my feet clambered a man—a living man. And behind him the light shone on the coffin as it lay at the bottom of the grave, shone on the lid that was partly wrenched off, shone on something brilliantly green that reposed within the coffin and whose repose had been about to be disturbed.

The man was St. Arnaud—a naturally living St. Arnaud.

I was bewildered—horrified and bewildered. I could not reason. I could do only one thing, and I did that. I sprang at St. Arnaud as he finally clambered out of the grave.

He met my onslaught, but I bore him down. In ordinary circumstances he might have defeated me, for he was wonderfully strong and agile for his age; but on my side I had sheer fury, and sheer fury won. He rose, and I bore him down again. Yet another time he struggled free; but now he was not fighting but merely trying to escape my blows; and at length I hit him fairly on the jaw—by accident, no doubt, for there was neither light nor room for anything but a cat-and-dog fight—and he tripped and fell headlong, crashing his head against the rugged corner of an ancient broken tombstone.

And at that very moment a piercing scream startled us and, turning, I saw that Leonora had risen quickly to her feet and was staring about her in horror.

I went round to her, while the doctor stepped over to St. Arnaud and shone his torch on the prone figure.

A moment later he came back.

"He's dead now, anyway," he said. "But I'm not going to certify the death this time."

He shone his light down into the grave. At that, Leonora, whom I had been supporting in my arms, turned to me with a cry of terror.

"I remember! I remember!" she exclaimed. "I remember everything now. That—that—down there—" she went on, her utterance broken by hysterical sobs, "—that's Miss Muller. He killed her—after I—He wasn't dead. He was alive—when they put him in the coffin. And he killed her—after I let him out. He was in a trance. He woke up in the night—and he called me. And I unscrewed the coffin, and he was alive. I remember everything now—everything. And we put Miss Muller's body into the coffin—and screwed it down again."

She was gesticulating wildly as she spoke. I doubt whether she knew what she was saying or who was listening to her. She was merely speaking her thoughts aloud, impelled by horror to express herself.

Then suddenly she ceased speaking, and before I could grip her she had fallen in a heap on the ground.

She had only fainted through the sheer violence of her emotions. And that was not to be wondered at, for my own feelings on hearing her horrible revelations were such as to make me think that I should never again know a moment's innocent happiness. I felt that the horror of Miss Muller's death would never leave me.

"There'll be the very devil to pay," said Dr. Bonner, as he and I knelt beside Leonora. "First, certifying as dead a man who isn't dead; then watching him open his own grave and not attempting to stop him; and then killing him in a fight. There'll be the very devil to pay!"

"We'll get out of it," I said, but I could not but appreciate the danger of our position.

"But it's this tragedy," he went on, nodding his head towards the grave, "that really matters. The inhuman monster!"

"And he attended the funeral," I said, suddenly recollecting the man who had introduced himself as Paul St. Arnaud's cousin.

And on that I became aware of the terrible danger in which we all had stood—living in a house in which a monster lurked, a monster lacking the crudest human feelings. I remembered the razor attack on myself. Leonora told me later that she knew nothing about that.

She opened her eyes.

"The book!" she said.

Then, seeing us, she recollected what had happened.

"What book?" I asked.

"Oh, it doesn't matter now," she said, with a sigh of infinite relief. "It's in there." She looked towards the grave. "We put some things in with the body—to make it heavier—and we put the book in, by mistake. The one with all his formulae. That's why we came here—to get it. He wanted it—after you destroyed that thing."

We managed, between us, to get Leonora back to Berner's Abbey but many days passed before she was able to take the slightest interest in her surroundings.

In the meantime Dr. Bonner's prediction that there would be the very devil to pay was amply fulfilled.

He and I found ourselves in the hands of the authorities, and we realized the enormity of our offence in allowing a grave to be opened. I was put on trial for having killed St. Arnaud, and to be finally acquitted was not such a simple matter as I had expected it to be. High medical authorities supported Dr. Bonner in his pleading against the charge of professional negligence which he had to answer during the inquiry into the facts of what was regarded as the most extraordinary affair within living memory, and he suffered no loss of prestige.

And what could we say to Major Muller and to the mother of the other girl who was murdered? We said all that human sympathy could say but that was poor consolation.

Yet we could not continue to dwell on the tragic side of these happenings, for us there was another side. For me there was the knowledge that Leonora was freed from the most frightful state of bondage that ever fell to the lot of a human being.

But before she could consent to marry me she insisted on my giving up all ideas of becoming a doctor. I understood and acquiesced.

THE END

MONKS' TOWER

MASTERMAN, HIS BACK TO THE FIRE, and a smile—half of bravado, half hesitation—on his face, looked at us, one after another, and said:

"I've a good mind to try it. Who's game?"

Angela Cressley, the only woman of the party gathered in the billiards-room, put a hand to her throat as though moved by fear. But at the same time there was a sparkle of doubt, of pleasurable, thrilling excitement, in her eyes.

"Oh, Bernard!" she said, looking up at Masterman. "What if—?"

She hesitated. We all looked at her. Some of us smiled; but some of us were serious—very serious. We had just been listening to stories of the ghost that was supposed to haunt this ancient Cumberland mansion, and the hour was late, and some of us had rooms that lay along distant corridors.

"What if there should be some truth it?" Angela Cressley managed to say.

Harry Cressley, Angela's husband, sneered.

"What about turning in?" he asked.

"Nobody game?" said the debonair Masterman, glancing round at us all again, but letting his gaze linger meaningly on Harry Cressley.

"You don't catch me losing a night's sleep for a bit of tomfoolery," said Harry, returning Masterman's taunting gaze in a markedly inimical manner.

"I wish I were a man," Angela murmured.

"Whether there be anything in it or not," said someone, "I shouldn't care to spend this particular night at the top of Monks' Tower. Listen to it! It's blowing like billy-ho!"

"Blusterous, certainly," Masterman agreed. "But this particular night happens to be the particular night on which some manifestation might be expected, as you've just heard."

His gaze was again resting on Harry Cressley.

"Lady Brenton might, not like it," said someone. "After all, it isn't our ghost; it's Lady Brenton's ghost."

"We can tell Lady Brenton in the morning," Masterman replied.

Angela Cressley's eyes had not left Masterman's face since he first suggested spending the night on Monks' Tower. There was in her expression something of delicious fear. And there was something, too, of hero-worship.

Had Angela been gifted with normal emotional stability she would have exclaimed, "It's all rubbish! Off to bed—all of you!" But she was the thoughtless, pretty-pretty kind of woman whom men foolishly die for.

"I wish I were a man," she repeated, letting her glance leave Masterman's handsome face and rest for a fateful moment on that of her middle-aged husband.

Harry Cressley was angry. I could see that. I could see it by the way in which he returned his wife's look. I could see it more plainly by the way in which he glanced at Masterman.

As I say, Harry Cressley was middle-aged, and Angela was young. She was young and foolish and pretty. And because she was pretty her husband was hungry for her regard. And because she was foolish she could amuse herself by keeping him uncertain of it.

In the present instance she was amusing herself by encouraging Bernard Masterman to undertake a somewhat spectacular enterprise—an enterprise that certainly needed some boldness—and she was thereby arousing her husband's jealousy, which flattered her immensely.

Yes, Harry Cressley was angry. But Masterman, courting cheap applause, could afford to overlook poor Harry's anger. Masterman had won the worship of the gallery, which was Angela.

"Well, I'm going up there to-night," he said, "even though I have to go alone . . . But don't the conditions make it clear that the watcher *should* be alone? Isn't, it the case that the ghost will never face more than one at a time—or some-thing of the sort?"

I saw Angela shudder. And certainly I had to admit that Masterman had pluck. Superstition, dread of the unknown, profound doubts, the instincts bred of millions of years— these are still with us; and when the imagination sets to work it is hard to cling to the rock of reason. It is difficult not to give way to doubts, then to fears, then to terror.

Yes, Masterman had pluck. There might be nothing in the legend that spoke of a ghost that haunted Monks' Tower, but on the other hand there might be something in it; and a man with any imagination at all would not lightly face the darkness and the loneliness of the battlemented top of the tower.

If only Angela had accepted this proof of Masterman's courage and sent us all off to bed! But she wanted the full delicious thrill out of the affair.

To her cheap vanity it meant much that the handsome Masterman should choose a night of discomfort in order to gain her applause, and that her husband—poor Harry— should be disturbed by doubts regarding his own ability to hold her respect.

I saw Harry look at his wife with a new expression. The anger had died out of his eyes. His glance was soft. He was in love with her. He valued her admiration, shallow though that might be.

The circumstances awakened the spirit of the jousting knight that lay beneath his rather prosaic appearance.

"I'll come with you," he said, carelessly. "It's a lot of dam tomfoolery, but—"

He paused, his lip curling into a sneer, and he was re-warded with a palpitating smile from Angela.

"I don't want to rob you of your place of honour on the battlements," he went on, crossing his legs and looking up at Masterman, who stood rocking himself on his heels with his back to the fire, "but I'll keep watch on the tower stair-case. The gibbering wraith goes up the staircase, I under-stand."

"It comes out of a room on the third gallery," someone said. "Where the body was kept preceding burial."

"Sometimes it comes from the churchyard," said some-one else.

I noticed several twinkling grins.

"Clad in the vestments of the tomb . . ." said a hollow voice at my elbow.

I turned my head and was met with a sly wink.

"Jaw bound, up . . ." said a young man, giving a mock shudder.

"Oh, don't be horrid!" Angela cried. She was inclined to be amused, but her amusement was very decidedly touched with fear. Possibly she did not believe in ghosts, but there are times when even the least superstitious allow doubts to trouble them.

Angela was not one of the least superstitious. She was thinking then, perhaps, that legends are not usually without some foundation in truth.

"I'll hang about on the ground floor," I put in, trying to laugh away my own uneasiness. "I'll be on hand to open the door for the visitant should it arrive from the church-yard," I added.

My regard for Harry induced me to make this decision. I was sorry for him.

He was being forced to face discomfort—if nothing worse—because of the whim of a foolish woman who hap-pened to be pretty. I thought I might help him to while away the long minutes of waiting—for minutes that mark a state of expectation seem interminable.

The gathering broke up and we all went to our rooms—the others to go to bed: Masterman, Harry Cressley and I to put on lounge suits and overcoats.

The general attitude was one of amusement. Had Masterman been going alone it might have been different; there would have been a certain amount of anxiety.

But the presence of three men in the tower gave the affair the atmosphere of a joke, as when serious-minded men in moments of relaxation do fantastically foolish things for wagers.

So all the others went to bed, generous in their advice to us regarding formulas for warding off the dire effects of the evil eye should it be exercised by a four centuries-old spectre. They also recommended rum for warding off the more dire effects of exposure to draughts on stone staircases at midnight.

Yes, they were all quite cheerful. Someone repeated the remark that Lady Brenton might not like it. For my part, I was of the opinion that she would be thoroughly amused when she should hear next morning of our escapade, though, for a moment, I had an uneasy feeling that she might be annoyed. It depended upon the authenticity or otherwise of the ghost.

In my room I changed hurriedly and put an electric torch in the pocket of my overcoat. Then I sauntered out and went along towards the room occupied by the Cressleys, intending to wait for Harry.

But with my hand outstretched to rattle a tattoo on the panels of their door, I hesitated. Harry and his wife were having a few words.

With the feelings of one in danger of being surprised in an ignoble act, I wandered off down the main staircase and in to the hall.

As there was still no sign either of Masterman or Harry, I made my way through the long, deserted corridors towards the disused part of the mansion from which that ancient edifice, the Monks' Tower, rose sixty feet into the blusterous night.

I could not, however, forget what I had heard when I approached the door of the

Cressleys' bedroom, and I realised that it would have been better for my immediate peace of mind had I not heard it.

Angela was crying. That was what had made me hesitate in the first place.

And, standing for a moment uncertainly, I had heard her exclaim: "But it's all rubbish, I tell you!"

Then I had heard Harry reply: "I wish I could honestly think so. But I know. I *know*. And it's your fault if anything happens—remember that!"

With these words repeating themselves my head, I was genuinely uneasy as I made my way towards the base of the Monks' Tower. Harry had spoken with conviction. Perhaps there was something the legend of the ghost, after all.

I knew Harry to be a solidly balanced sort of man, and when he gave an opinion it was usually one that had some authority behind it. He knew something about this ghost— that I could not doubt. "I know. I *know*. And it's your fault if anything happens."

And now I saw the full measure of his courage. As I went along the echoing vaults that were the corridors, the light from my torch making them seem only the more hollow and, ghostly, I reflected that Harry was the braver of the two men.

Masterman, it seemed, was only acting the showman, to gain the admiration of a pretty woman; but Harry, to retain the respect of that same pretty woman, was knowingly courting danger—it might be, death.

As for me, I was certainly wishing that the night were over.

I reached the hall that is at the base of the Monks' Tower. The vast cavern—icy cold like a tomb—echoed to my hesitating footsteps. I shone my torch around.

The light made panelling and pictures and dusty pieces of ancient furniture spring forward into prominence, then recede out of sight as the darkness swallowed them up again.

I shone my torch upwards, but it failed to illuminate the higher galleries, which remained shrouded in mystery and gloom.

And now I heard footsteps, and presently the sweeping beams from the torches of my companions came out of the cavernous distance; Masterman and Harry, in hats, coats and mufflers, appeared and stepped towards me.

I greeted them in a hushed voice.

"All right!" said Harry, laughing.

"No need to make it worse than it is. You won't wake the dead, however loudly you might speak."

But his laugh did not ring true.

"And we shan't wake the living, either," I commented, "however loudly we might shout. The inhabited part of the mansion is a long way off."

We stood chatting together for a moment or two; then Harry took Masterman's arm and they walked towards the staircase. I thought that Masterman did not seem so sure of himself as he had been.

"I'll take your place on the battlements, if you like," Harry said—earnestly I thought.

Masterman, giving an unnecessarily forceful laugh, dismissed the suggestion.

"Shall we keep our torches on?" Harry then suggested.

I could see that he was grimly aware of the seriousness of the business, but that he did not wish to arouse our fears.

"No!" said Masterman, with an oath. "A fine thing—tomorrow! When we tell them that we had to burn lights to keep the ghost away!"

I watched them as they started to ascend the stone staircase—the middle aged Harry Cressley, undistinguished in build and manner, and the broad shouldered Masterman, still under forty and at the peak of physical perfection.

When they reached the first gallery, which ran across one side of the hollow tower, I switched off my torch and started to pace about in the darkness, shivering slightly with the cold and not envying Masterman his situation out on the battlements, for the violent wind beat in gusts upon the tower and moaned and whined about the great oaken door and the barred and leaded windows,

The door! Someone had said that the ghost sometimes came to the tower from the churchyard. An invention of the moment, of course! In any case, the door was solid enough, and I had seen the massive bolts that were shot into their massive sockets. Yet, ghosts took no account of locks and bolts—or even of oaken doors.

Surely I was beginning to dither! I laughed.

By this time my two companions were far above me. I could see them as black silhouettes against the beams of their torches while they moved, up the flights of stairs or round the galleries by which the climb was interrupted.

Presently they stopped. And after the space of a few moments one torch went on alone. And when that had vanished through a door at the very top—sixty feet above me—the other torch, on the third gallery, went out and we were left to utter darkness and the intermittent moaning and shrieking of the night wind.

And now my imagination came into play. The time was close on twelve o'clock; and such was the immediate effect of the sinister darkness with which I was surrounded that I actually imagined the hour to have significance.

I caught myself stopping in my stride and listening for some sound that would be distinct from the moan and shriek of the wind; and when I resumed my pacing I was glancing this way and that in fear lest I might see something—something in the vestments of the tomb, as someone had said—evolve out of the darkness of this icy cavern.

Though I was ashamed of my nervous alertness, I could not force myself to be calm and detached. Everything contributed to induce expectancy. All the superstitious doubts that had ever filled primitive man with terror came to my mind.

My imagination rejected reason, so that I had to allow that there might be some truth in the legends of earthly survival after death. That there *must* be some truth in them! Wiser men than I had preached that gospel.

The woman—for it was a woman for whom we were waiting, a woman done to death by the monks four centuries ago by being thrown from this tower—the woman might appear, and human reason could not guess what might happen then.

I had thought that Harry Cressley and I, at least, would have some comfort from the sense of each other's presence; but Harry, on the third gallery, seemed a long way off. I could neither see him nor hear him. Anything might happen to him—or to me.

And as for Masterman, who was out on the battlements . . .

Harry Cressley, I knew, must be near the door of the small room from which the ghost was supposed to emerge. If time and space meant anything in the spirit world, he would probably be the first to be aware of the ghost's presence.

The legend said that the form ascended to the battlements. And anybody found there was doomed. Fear drove such a person to fling himself out into space. Presumably certain death in that fashion was preferable to the horror of being touched by a wraith.

And, incidentally, such an end was a fitting form of vengeance on the part of the ghost, for the woman herself had been murdered by being thrown from the top of the tower.

I laughed at myself for trying to make the legend acceptable to reason. For, of course, it was only an escapade—a jest—this watching for a ghost.

Yet, Harry had said that he wished he could honestly think it was all rubbish; that he knew—he *knew*; and that it would be Angela's fault if anything were to happen.

And something *did* happen.

I was peering upwards into the darkness, trying to distinguish the form of Harry among the multitude of shadows that made the interior of the tower almost totally black. I was thinking about calling up to him to make sure that he was all right. A few cheerful words might make the gloom more bearable.

But it was Harry who spoke first. Not cheerful words, however. At his hoarse cry I switched on my torch and shone it upwards. I could see him leaning over the third gallery, and even in the faint light that reached him I saw horror written on his face.

I did not wait to try to make out what he was saying. His gibbering attempts at speech were enough; the words did not matter. I dashed up the stairs and along the galleries, round and round, breathlessly.

Harry, when I reached him, was standing at his post, staring upwards towards tile little door that led out to the flat roof. He was trembling. He was mumbling to himself. He seemed to be only half aware of my presence.

" It went up there," he managed to say when I gripped him firmly and asked him what had happened. "You saw it? . . . Listen! Masterman—screaming!"

I did not stop to listen. In any case the howling of the wind and its violent buffeting against the tower made such a confusion of sound that a cry from the battlements would hardly be distinguished.

"Come on!" I cried, shaking Harry roughly to make him take a grip on himself.

He followed, still mumbling incoherently, as I rushed up to the top of the tower. Strangely enough, I was not afraid. Action and excitement precluded fear.

But on the last flight of the stairs I paused. It might be that Harry had only imagined the ghost, I reflected. The darkness and the long period of expectant waiting had begun to play upon his nerves. And to dash excitedly on to the roof and be confronted by a calm, supercilious Masterman would be somewhat mortifying.

But there was justification for my excitement. I learnt that in a very few moments. Masterman was gone!

The screaming wind met us as we stumbled through the doorway and emerged on to the flat, exposed roof, and for a second or two I was choked and beaten back by the fierce gusts. I remember wondering whether a spirit—a thing immaterial, lighter than air—could resist the force of a wind such as that. But, oddly enough, I gave little thought to the ghost.

Masterman was gone!

The top of the tower was not more than twenty feet square and held no projections that might conceal anyone. In a matter of seconds the beam of my torch had lighted up every corner.

Harry was holding on to the doorpost, but whether from fear or from inability to stand up to the gale I did not know.

I hurried him inside again. His nerve seemed to be gone. I was sorry for him even while I was swearing at him to pull himself together. I wondered whether I should have had such control over myself had *I* seen the wraith. I could understand his nerves going to pieces. And his sensibilities were perhaps more acute than mine, so that this horror struck him more deeply.

For one thing, he had been able to distinguish Masterman's cry of terror while we were still down on the third gallery; fear had sharpened his senses.

My thoughts were not with ghosts now; they were with Masterman. I was sure that we should find him lying on the gravel at the foot of the tower, as people had formerly been found.

And that is where we *did* find him—a horrible sight!

The jest had ended tragically. The legends were true, and ghosts still walked.

Such were the frightful thoughts that made me stand, horror-struck, while others whom we had aroused came to our assistance. Masterman, in panic, had gone back over the battlements and into space when faced with a wraith advancing towards him!

The rest of the scene out there in the darkness is a confused jumble in my mind . . .

The next thing I remember is that I was in my own room, sipping whisky.

A faint knock came at my door.

"Who's that?" I cried, jumping to my feet.

"May I come in, old chap?"

The door opened and a white-faced young man in a dressing-gown slipped inside. He was one of the youngest members of the house-party. His manner showed a fearful concern. He was breathing rapidly and his staring eyes held mine.

"Did you see it?" he asked, breathlessly.

"Why, what's the matter?" I said, alarmed.

"Excuse me, old chap," he murmured. "I had to come to see you. I don't know what to do. It's about Mrs. Cressley . . ."

He did not ask permission, but walked to the door and turned the key in the lock. Then he came back and sat down on the bed.

"But what about Mrs. Cressley?" I demanded, urgently. "What's happened to *her*?"

"Well—" he began, then paused.

"I don't know what to do," he repeated. "I must tell somebody. And you're the one to tell. You were there. You saw the ghost."

"Anyhow, what the dickens are you talking about?" I asked.

Then he blurted it all out.

Sitting somewhere on the previous day—on the library floor, poring over some books, I think he said—he had been forced to listen to something that was not intended for his ears.

He had heard Masterman and Mrs. Cressley talking about passports, and it had come out unmistakably that these two were on the point of making a bolt to the Continent. It was much more involved than that, but the central fact stood out clearly.

Then I saw what was on his mind.

"I intended to warn Cressley," he said. " I ought to have done it to-night. But I put it off. Not a thing one would take a pleasure in doing. I put it off. I made up my mind to tell him first thing in the morning—definitely.

"But now this has happened. Masterman, I mean, being killed. Do you think Cressley knew—about Mrs. Cressley and Masterman?

"Oh, no!" he went on hurriedly, rising from the bed and taking one or two nervous steps about the floor. "I didn't mean to suggest that. Harry Cressley couldn't—Did you see it? That's what I came to ask. Did *you* see the ghost?"

I stared at him in horror. He moved uneasily under my gaze. He thought I was angry—outraged—at the suggestion that Harry Cressley might have murdered the man who was going to rob him of his wife.

But I was not angry. I was not thinking of that. I was thinking of Angela crying in her bedroom and saying, "But it's all rubbish, I tell you!" And I was thinking of Harry's reply: "I wish I could honestly think so. But I know. I *know*. And it's your fault if anything happens."

This was what Harry had known. He knew nothing of the truth of legends or of the authenticity of ghosts. But this: that Masterman was going to rob him of his wife.

"Yes," I said, and I was amazed at my own coolness; "I *did* see the ghost. A woman. In white. She came out of one of the rooms on the third gallery and seemed to drift up to the top of the tower. Then we heard Masterman shriek. But he was gone before we could reach him . . ."

It seems that in, moments of high emotion one's sympathies are thrown violently into one side of the scale or the other. Neither reason nor right holds the balance. But I doubt whether reason or right would have induced me to hand Harry over to the hangman.

Exemplary citizens might not comprehend me.

RAMBLE HOUSE's

HARRY STEPHEN KEELER WEBWORK MYSTERIES

(RH) indicates the title is available ONLY in the RAMBLE HOUSE edition

Keeler Related Works

A To Izzard: A Harry Stephen Keeler Companion by Fender Tucker — Articles and stories about Harry, by Harry, and in his style. Included is a compleat bibliography.

Wild About Harry: Reviews of Keeler Novels — Edited by Richard Polt & Fender Tucker — 22 reviews of works by Harry Stephen Keeler from *Keeler News*. A perfect introduction to the author.

The Keeler Keyhole Collection: Annotated newsletter rants from Harry Stephen Keeler, edited by Francis M. Nevins. Over 400 pages of incredibly personal Keeleriana.

Fakealoo — Pastiches of the style of Harry Stephen Keeler by selected demented members of the HSK Society. Updated every year with the new winner.

RAMBLE HOUSE's OTHER LOONS

The End of It All and Other Stories — Ed Gorman's latest short story collection

Four Dancing Tuatara Press Books — *Beast or Man?* By Sean M'Guire; *The Whistling Ancestors* by Richard E. Goddard; *The Shadow on the House* and *Sorcerer's Chessmen* by Mark Hansom. With introductions by John Pelan

The Dumpling — Political murder from 1907 by Coulson Kernahan

Victims & Villains — Intriguing Sherlockiana from Derham Groves

Evidence in Blue — 1938 mystery by E. Charles Vivian

The Case of the Little Green Men — Mack Reynolds wrote this love song to sci-fi fans back in 1951 and it's now back in print.

Hell Fire — A new hard-boiled novel by Jack Moskovitz about an arsonist, an arson cop and a Nazi hooker. It isn't pretty.

Researching American-Made Toy Soldiers — A 276-page collection of a lifetime of articles by toy soldier expert Richard O'Brien

Strands of the Web: Short Stories of Harry Stephen Keeler — Edited and Introduced by Fred Cleaver

The Sam McCain Novels — Ed Gorman's terrific series includes *The Day the Music Died, Wake Up Little Susie* and *Will You Still Love Me Tomorrow?*

A Shot Rang Out — Three decades of reviews from Jon Breen

Mysterious Martin, the Master of Murder — Two versions of a strange 1912 novel by Tod Robbins about a man who writes books that can kill.

Dago Red — 22 tales of dark suspense by Bill Pronzini

The Night Remembers — A 1991 Jack Walsh mystery from Ed Gorman

Rough Cut & New, Improved Murder — Ed Gorman's first two novels

Hollywood Dreams — A novel of the Depression by Richard O'Brien

Seven Gelett Burgess Novels — *The Master of Mysteries, The White Cat, Two O'Clock Courage, Ladies in Boxes, Find the Woman, The Heart Line, The Picaroons*

The Organ Reader — A huge compilation of just about everything published in the 1971-1972 radical bay-area newspaper, *THE ORGAN*.

A Clear Path to Cross — Sharon Knowles short mystery stories by Ed Lynskey

Old Times' Sake — Short stories by James Reasoner from Mike Shayne Magazine

Freaks and Fantasies — Eerie tales by Tod Robbins, collaborator of Tod Browning on the film FREAKS.

Seven Jim Harmon Double Novels — *Vixen Hollow/Celluloid Scandal, The Man Who Made Maniacs/Silent Siren, Ape Rape/Wanton Witch, Sex Burns Like Fire/Twist Session, Sudden Lust/Passion Strip, Sin Unlimited/Harlot Master, Twilight Girls/Sex Institution.* Written in the early 60s.

Marblehead: A Novel of H.P. Lovecraft — A long-lost masterpiece from Richard A. Lupoff. Published for the first time!

The Compleat Ova Hamlet — Parodies of SF authors by Richard A. Lupoff – A brand new edition with more stories and more illustrations by Trina Robbins.

The Secret Adventures of Sherlock Holmes — Three Sherlockian pastiches by the Brooklyn author/publisher, Gary Lovisi.

The Universal Holmes — Richard A. Lupoff's 2007 collection of five Holmesian pastiches and a recipe for giant rat stew.

Four Joel Townsley Rogers Novels — By the author of *The Red Right Hand: Once In a Red Moon, Lady With the Dice, The Stopped Clock, Never Leave My Bed*

Two Joel Townsley Rogers Story Collections — Night of Horror and Killing Time

Twenty Norman Berrow Novels — *The Bishop's Sword, Ghost House, Don't Go Out After Dark, Claws of the Cougar, The Smokers of Hashish, The Secret Dancer, Don't Jump Mr. Boland!, The Footprints of Satan, Fingers for Ransom, The Three Tiers of Fantasy, The Spaniard's Thumb, The Eleventh Plague, Words Have Wings, One Thrilling Night, The Lady's in Danger, It Howls at Night, The Terror in the Fog, Oil Under the Window, Murder in the Melody, The Singing Room*

The N. R. De Mexico Novels — Robert Bragg presents *Marijuana Girl, Madman on a Drum, Private Chauffeur* in one volume.

Four Chelsea Quinn Yarbro Novels featuring Charlie Moon — *Ogilvie, Tallant and Moon, Music When the Sweet Voice Dies, Poisonous Fruit* and *Dead Mice*

Five Walter S. Masterman Mysteries — *The Green Toad, The Flying Beast, The Yellow Mistletoe, The Wrong Verdict* and *The Perjured Alibi.* Fantastic impossible plots.

Two Hake Talbot Novels — *Rim of the Pit, The Hangman's Handyman.* Classic locked room mysteries.

Two Alexander Laing Novels — *The Motives of Nicholas Holtz* and *Dr. Scarlett,* stories of medical mayhem and intrigue from the 30s.

Four David Hume Novels — *Corpses Never Argue, Cemetery First Stop, Make Way for the Mourners, Eternity Here I Come,* and more to come.

Three Wade Wright Novels — *Echo of Fear, Death At Nostalgia Street* and *It Leads to Murder,* with more to come!

Eight Rupert Penny Novels — *Policeman's Holiday, Policeman's Evidence, Lucky Policeman, Policeman in Armour, Sealed Room Murder, Sweet Poison, The Talkative Policeman, She had to Have Gas* and *Cut and Run* (by Martin Tanner.)

Five Jack Mann Novels — Strange murder in the English countryside. *Gees' First Case, Nightmare Farm, Grey Shapes, The Ninth Life, The Glass Too Many.*

Seven Max Afford Novels — *Owl of Darkness, Death's Mannikins, Blood on His Hands, The Dead Are Blind, The Sheep and the Wolves, Sinners in Paradise* and *Two Locked Room Mysteries and a Ripping Yarn* by one of Australia's finest novelists.

Five Joseph Shallit Novels — *The Case of the Billion Dollar Body, Lady Don't Die on My Doorstep, Kiss the Killer, Yell Bloody Murder, Take Your Last Look.* One of America's best 50's authors.

Two Crimson Clown Novels — By Johnston McCulley, author of the Zorro novels, *The Crimson Clown* and *The Crimson Clown Again.*

The Best of 10-Story Book — edited by Chris Mikul, over 35 stories from the literary magazine Harry Stephen Keeler edited.

A Young Man's Heart — A forgotten early classic by Cornell Woolrich

The Anthony Boucher Chronicles — edited by Francis M. Nevins
Book reviews by Anthony Boucher written for the *San Francisco Chronicle,* 1942 – 1947. Essential and fascinating reading.

Muddled Mind: Complete Works of Ed Wood, Jr. — David Hayes and Hayden Davis deconstruct the life and works of a mad genius.

Gadsby — A lipogram (a novel without the letter E). Ernest Vincent Wright's last work, published in 1939 right before his death.

My First Time: The One Experience You Never Forget — Michael Birchwood — 64 true first-person narratives of how they lost it.

A Roland Daniel Double: The Signal and The Return of Wu Fang — Classic thrillers from the 30s

Murder in Shawnee — Two novels of the Alleghenies by John Douglas: *Shawnee Alley Fire* and *Haunts.*

Deep Space and other Stories — A collection of SF gems by Richard A. Lupoff

Blood Moon — The first of the Robert Payne series by Ed Gorman

The Time Armada — Fox B. Holden's 1953 SF gem.

Black River Falls — Suspense from the master, Ed Gorman

Sideslip — 1968 SF masterpiece by Ted White and Dave Van Arnam

The Triune Man — Mindscrambling science fiction from Richard A. Lupoff

Detective Duff Unravels It — Episodic mysteries by Harvey O'Higgins

Automaton — Brilliant treatise on robotics: 1928-style! By H. Stafford Hatfield

The Incredible Adventures of Rowland Hern — Rousing 1928 impossible crimes by Nicholas Olde.

Slammer Days — Two full-length prison memoirs: *Men into Beasts* (1952) by George Sylvester Viereck and *Home Away From Home* (1962) by Jack Woodford

Murder in Black and White — 1931 classic tennis whodunit by Evelyn Elder

Killer's Caress — Cary Moran's 1936 hardboiled thriller

The Golden Dagger — 1951 Scotland Yard yarn by E. R. Punshon

A Smell of Smoke — 1951 English countryside thriller by Miles Burton

Ruled By Radio — 1925 futuristic novel by Robert L. Hadfield & Frank E. Farncombe

Murder in Silk — A 1937 Yellow Peril novel of the silk trade by Ralph Trevor

The Case of the Withered Hand — 1936 potboiler by John G. Brandon

Finger-prints Never Lie — A 1939 classic detective novel by John G. Brandon

Inclination to Murder — 1966 thriller by New Zealand's Harriet Hunter

Invaders from the Dark — Classic werewolf tale from Greye La Spina

Fatal Accident — Murder by automobile, a 1936 mystery by Cecil M. Wills

The Devil Drives — A prison and lost treasure novel by Virgil Markham

Dr. Odin — Douglas Newton's 1933 potboiler comes back to life.

The Chinese Jar Mystery — Murder in the manor by John Stephen Strange, 1934

The Julius Caesar Murder Case — A classic 1935 re-telling of the assassination by Wallace Irwin that's much more fun than the Shakespeare version

West Texas War and Other Western Stories — by Gary Lovisi

The Contested Earth and Other SF Stories — A never-before published space opera and seven short stories by Jim Harmon.

Tales of the Macabre and Ordinary — Modern twisted horror by Chris Mikul, author of the *Bizarrism* series.

The Gold Star Line — Seaboard adventure from L.T. Reade and Robert Eustace.

The Werewolf vs the Vampire Woman — Hard to believe ultraviolence by either Arthur M. Scarm or Arthur M. Scram.

Black Hogan Strikes Again — Australia's Peter Renwick pens a tale of the outback.

Don Diablo: Book of a Lost Film — Two-volume treatment of a western by Paul Landres, with diagrams. Intro by Francis M. Nevins.

The Charlie Chaplin Murder Mystery — Movie hijinks by Wes D. Gehring

The Koky Comics — A collection of all of the 1978-1981 Sunday and daily comic strips by Richard O'Brien and Mort Gerberg, in two volumes.

Suzy — Another collection of comic strips from Richard O'Brien and Bob Vojtko

Dime Novels: Ramble House's 10-Cent Books — *Knife in the Dark* by Robert Leslie Bellem, *Hot Lead* and *Song of Death* by Ed Earl Repp, *A Hashish House in New York* by H.H. Kane, and five more.

Blood in a Snap — The *Finnegan's Wake* of the 21st century, by Jim Weiler

Stakeout on Millennium Drive — Award-winning Indianapolis Noir — Ian Woollen.

Dope Tales #1 — Two dope-riddled classics; *Dope Runners* by Gerald Grantham and *Death Takes the Joystick* by Phillip Condé.

Dope Tales #2 — Two more narco-classics; *The Invisible Hand* by Rex Dark and *The Smokers of Hashish* by Norman Berrow.

Dope Tales #3 — Two enchanting novels of opium by the master, Sax Rohmer. *Dope* and *The Yellow Claw*.

Tenebrae — Ernest G. Henham's 1898 horror tale brought back.

The Singular Problem of the Stygian House-Boat — Two classic tales by John Kendrick Bangs about the denizens of Hades.

Tiresias — Psychotic modern horror novel by Jonathan M. Sweet.

The One After Snelling — Kickass modern noir from Richard O'Brien.

The Sign of the Scorpion — 1935 Edmund Snell tale of oriental evil.

The House of the Vampire — 1907 poetic thriller by George S. Viereck.

An Angel in the Street — Modern hardboiled noir by Peter Genovese.

The Devil's Mistress — Scottish gothic tale by J. W. Brodie-Innes.

The Lord of Terror — 1925 mystery with master-criminal, Fantômas.

The Lady of the Terraces — 1925 adventure by E. Charles Vivian.

My Deadly Angel — 1955 Cold War drama by John Chelton

Prose Bowl — Futuristic satire — Bill Pronzini & Barry N. Malzberg .

Satan's Den Exposed — True crime in Truth or Consequences New Mexico — Award-winning journalism by the *Desert Journal*.

The Amorous Intrigues & Adventures of Aaron Burr — by Anonymous — Hot historical action.

I Stole $16,000,000 — A true story by cracksman Herbert E. Wilson.

The Black Dark Murders — Vintage 50s college murder yarn by Milt Ozaki, writing as Robert O. Saber.

Sex Slave — Potboiler of lust in the days of Cleopatra — Dion Leclercq.

You'll Die Laughing — Bruce Elliott's 1945 novel of murder at a practical joker's English countryside manor.

The Private Journal & Diary of John H. Surratt — The memoirs of the man who conspired to assassinate President Lincoln.

Dead Man Talks Too Much — Hollywood boozer by Weed Dickenson

Red Light — History of legal prostitution in Shreveport Louisiana by Eric Brock. Includes wonderful photos of the houses and the ladies.

A Snark Selection — Lewis Carroll's *The Hunting of the Snark* with two Snarkian chapters by Harry Stephen Keeler — Illustrated by Gavin L. O'Keefe.

Ripped from the Headlines! — The Jack the Ripper story as told in the newspaper articles in the *New York* and *London Times*.

Geronimo — S. M. Barrett's 1905 autobiography of a noble American.

The White Peril in the Far East — Sidney Lewis Gulick's 1905 indictment of the West and assurance that Japan would never attack the U.S.

The Compleat Calhoon — All of Fender Tucker's works: Includes *Totah Six-Pack*, *Weed, Women and Song* and *Tales from the Tower*, plus a CD of all of his songs.

Totah Six-Pack — Just Fender Tucker's six tales about Farmington in one sleek volume.

RAMBLE HOUSE
Fender Tucker, Prop.
www.ramblehouse.com   fender@ramblehouse.com
228-826-1783   10329 Sheephead Drive, Vancleave MS 39565

www.ingramcontent.com/pod-product-compliance
Lightning Source LLC
Chambersburg PA
CBHW030328020726
47493CB00004B/1201